A MIND
DISEASED

A MIND DISEASED

CATHERINE MOLONEY

ROBERT HALE

First published in 2019 by
Robert Hale, an imprint of
The Crowood Press Ltd,
Ramsbury, Marlborough
Wiltshire SN8 2HR

www.crowood.com

British Library Cataloguing-in-Publication Data
A catalogue record for this book is available from the
British Library.

ISBN 978 0 7198 2902 4

Typeset by Chapter One Book Production, Knebworth

Printed and bound in India by Replika Press Pvt Ltd

CONTENTS

To the Highlanders,
C, C and I

PROLOGUE

BLIMEY, THAT LAST STRETCH was a bugger. I'm getting too old for this.

Ernie Roberts stood doubled over at the top of Bromgrove Rise on a raw Sunday afternoon in January, struggling to get his breath back. Finally, he straightened up and headed across to the bench whose lofty pre-eminence afforded panoramic views across Bromgrove Woods below.

Gently, Ernie ran his fingers over the bench's little bronze memorial plaque.

In loving memory of Jean Roberts who loved this place.

'Hello, luv,' he wheezed. 'I made it. Reckon I'll be glad of that pint in the Shoulder of Mutton once I get back down.'

Sitting down heavily, he looked about him.

I'm the king of the world.

Most Bromgrove folk found the Rise too bleak, with its undulating stretches of furze, gorse and heather criss-crossed by winding sandy paths. But Ernie never tired of watching the kaleidoscope play of the light across the shrubs and wild grasses, turning them into a mysterious ever-shifting sea so that he half expected to see Neptune or some other watery deity rise with a trident from their depths.

Jean used to tease him for his poetical streak. 'Fey, that's what you are,' she told him. But he knew she felt it too. Their own private kingdom, where they escaped into another world inaccessible to the soulless sing song tannoy of the Bestway Cash and Carry where Jean had worked on the tills or the endless refrain of rickety trolleys in the Newman Hospital which seemed to ring in his ears even after the day's portering was done.

He inhaled deeply, filling his lungs with the cold sharp air, wiping the week's slate clean.

Looking down towards the thickly clustering woods over-hung by a blood-red sun, Ernie smiled as he watched Waffle scurrying in and out of spongy banks and rank thickets.

Typical terrier. On the scent of God only knew what. Daft name for a dog really. But Jean had insisted ...

He must have lost himself for a bit. The light seemed to be growing wan, and wreaths of mist were rising from the ground like ghostly exhalations.

Time to make a move. Somewhat stiff now, Ernie heaved himself to his feet.

Again, he ran his fingers over the plaque in valediction before heading back down the gravel track which skirted the edge of the woods.

'C'mon, Waffle,' he called. 'Home time.'

Suddenly, the little terrier erupted from the underbrush barking, as Ernie later said, like something possessed.

Alternately circling Ernie and darting backwards and for-wards to the adjacent copse, Waffle clearly had something she wanted to show him.

Oh God. A rotting carcass or some such. Guaranteed to put him right off his pint ...

Gingerly, he advanced into the copse. It felt oppressive after the crisp freedom of the hilltop.

Too many stifling trees.

In that instant, he very much wanted to be away from the gloom and the spiralling mist which seemed to stalk him like a footpad.

'C'mon, girl,' he said hoarsely. 'Whatever it is, it can wait. We—'

Whatever Ernie had meant to say remained unsaid, his heart beating twice as fast as normal.

Waffle was dancing around what was recognizably a skeletonized human arm and hand sticking out of a clump of undergrowth.

Afterwards, Ernie thought how absurd it was that he had tiptoed forwards as though this was some fairy story and he was afraid to waken the sleeper in the forest.

This wasn't like the forests of childhood, where playing and singing would echo through the trees and the dense foliage was touched with enchantment.

This was a place where something unspeakably evil had happened.

Murder.

Most of the skeleton was there in the tangled scrub.

With the detached, rational part of his mind, he wondered how long it had taken for the body to decompose to bones and whether animals had made off with the rest.

Was it foxes? Or rats? Did they fight over the body? Did they tear it to shreds?

How come nobody found it until now?

Why *him*?

Suddenly, the hairs rose on the back of Ernie's neck, as though there was a shadowy figure watching the scene with him. *Gloating.*

He spun round, checking every murky patch of foliage.

No-one.

Slowly, he turned back to the remains.

Waffle was quiet now, spooked like him.

A wave of crushing pity washed over Ernie.

Wasn't it enough to kill the poor soul, without dumping the corpse like this out in the open, exposed to the elements, at the mercy of scavengers?

The ultimate indignity.

Along with the pity, Ernie felt a surge of hatred so strong it nearly choked him.

Jean's memorial was defiled. Her magical kingdom polluted by something unspeakable.

Bending down, with shaking hands he put the leash on a now subdued Waffle.

Then he fumbled for his mobile.

1

A Voice from the Grave

A MISTY MONDAY MORNING. Another bench. This time, the back of Bromgrove Police Station where DI Gilbert Markham sat enjoying a moment of tranquillity.

It was always like this at the start of a case. The need to fill himself with total stillness before the mayhem of the investigation took over.

Markham felt almost as though he wasn't even breathing. Almost as though he'd become part of some municipal phantasmagoria rather than a city of bricks and mortar.

There in front of him was the blackened Victorian pile of the Town Hall. Behind that rose the ancient terraces of St Chad's cemetery on one side and Hollingrove Park with its gentle contours on the other.

A view as familiar to him as his own face. A view he had contemplated thousands of times before.

And yet now, by some mysterious alchemy, subtly different.

The alchemy of murder.

In the stillness, Markham felt he was absorbing everything around him with clinical detachment, with no conscious thought at all. Observation, but no observer. A vibrant, alert hyper-awareness.

If he listened hard enough, he would hear voices pulsating through the landscape, pushing back the walls of time. The voices of those 'dunged with rotten death' who cried out to be avenged.

With one long, last look, the DI got up and made his way round to the main entrance and the lift which would whisk him to CID.

Early as it was, two familiar faces awaited him.

DS George Noakes was sprawled across his work station wolfing down what looked like a McDonald's double sausage and egg McMuffin, watched by DS Kate Burton of whose appalled expression he was happily oblivious.

It was an amusing study in contrasts. The grizzled, frowsy veteran and the bright-as-a-button university graduate.

Despite the DCI's best efforts, Markham had stubbornly resisted all attempts to prise George Noakes from his side. He couldn't do his job without the other's unvarnished honesty, common sense and bloody-minded disregard for social conventions. It was as simple as that. Rarely as they shared personal confidences, the DI knew that no man's metal rang as true as Noakes's, and that they somehow understood each other at a level beyond words. Wherever their investigations took them, whatever treacherous shoals and quicksands they had to navigate, he knew the DS had his back, 'though hell should bar the way'. 'The bizarrest bromance,' Markham's teacher girlfriend Olivia Mullen was wont to chuckle, but she had a soft spot for Noakes who reciprocated in kind, regarding his boss's willowy red-haired partner with a reverential awe which was proof against any amount of disapproval from 'the missus' or ribbing by colleagues.

Queasily, with intimations of nausea circling round her digestive system, Kate Burton observed her fellow DS gobble down the last greasy morsel of his McMuffin. A contented post-prandial belch indicated that it had lived up (or should that be down?) to expectations.

With a sardonic glance at Noakes, the DI headed for his glassed-in corner office with unrivalled views of the station car park. Snatching up her notebook, Burton was quick to follow while Noakes took one last slurp of his coffee and lobbed the plastic cup in the direction of his waste basket, not appearing unduly concerned when it missed.

Markham gave the radiator in his freezing office a half-hearted thump, as if by that means he could galvanize the temperamental heating system into action. Then he sat down behind his desk, waving his two subordinates to chairs opposite.

As ever, Noakes's working ensemble seemed positively calculated to induce a migraine, the virulent mustard jacket and candy stripe shirt straining over baggy chinos the colour of shredded wheat. The dazzling effect of a Royal British Legion tie was significantly diminished by a large blob of ketchup smack in the middle, while the overall look was best described as dragged through a hedge backwards. Watching him chomping away at his coronary-in-a-carton, only breaking off for slugs of coffee, Markham had sent up a silent prayer of thanks that DCI Sidney's quarters were two floors up so that he was unlikely ever to witness such Lucullan debauches. As it was, the DS's continued presence in CID was a running sore to Sidney, or Slimy Sid as he was more popularly known. 'He'll drag you down, you mark my words,' went the perennial refrain. 'Looks like a slob, and as for interpersonal skills ... the diversity people just throw up their hands in horror. The sooner we can put him out to grass, the better. I mean, *Noakes*, the face of modern policing! It's a sick joke!'

'Well, *was* it him, Guv? The doc?' Noakes asked.

Burton leaned forward, eager to hear the answer.

'Yes, it was, Noakes. Doctor Jonathan Warr, consultant psychiatrist at the Newman Hospital. Missing for nearly a year. Until now, not a trace, nothing. The smart money was on him having experienced some kind of breakdown or amnesiac episode. And there had been rumours of marital strain and stress at work, not least because of an ongoing investigation by the General Medical Council and Care Quality Commission into allegations of patient abuse at the facility. All in all, more than enough to tip even a well-respected professional over the edge.'

'But this breakdown business is only a theory, innit, Guv?'

'Yes, only a theory. Another theory is that Doctor Warr disappeared to start a new life, though there were no leads to indicate whether he had tried to fake his own death or had experienced a protracted fugue state which led to him walking out. Anyway, whatever the truth of the matter, it's definitely Doctor Warr,' said Markham quietly. 'Dental records confirm it. And there were some scraps of clothing.'

'How come no-one found the body till now?' Noakes was puzzled. 'I mean, isn't Bromley Woods where all the dog walkers and fitness freaks hang out?'

'There would have been two feet or so of water when Doctor Warr was dumped there ... probably around last March.'

Doctor Warr. For Markham, the dead were never anonymous, and he was notoriously intolerant of any approach to gallows humour. Junior officers had learned the hard way to avoid any off-colour remarks around the austere DI whose gaze could freeze a subordinate at ten paces.

'A watercourse, sir?' Burton tried to visualize the

topography. 'So, that would have made decomposition happen faster? Does this mean he died at the same time as he disappeared? What about—'

A snort from Noakes brought her up short. She blushed.

DS Burton's nut-brown pageboy hairdo gleamed like an advertisement for L'Oréal, while alert brown eyes watched everything from under her neat fringe with the air of an intelligent beagle. A well-cut charcoal trouser suit, immaculate white shirt and highly polished black ankle boots all proclaimed that this was a young officer going places, while her work station, streamlined within an inch of its life, could not have presented a greater contrast with that of her dishevelled neighbour.

Although not exactly pretty, Kate Burton's retroussé nose and neat features were not without a certain charm. Keenly intelligent and ambitious, there had been resistance from home when she joined the force so her police career had not been plain sailing, whatever Noakes said about fast-track graduates and silver spoons.

Having worked together on an earlier case which led to Burton's permanent promotion to CID (via an MA in Gender Studies at Bromgrove University), an uneasy truce had formed between her and Noakes. In some strange way, their widely differing personalities complemented each other, though the old war horse's un-PC pronouncements were still capable of raising her hackles. Most of the time, however, she refused to rise to the bait.

Deep inside, though unacknowledged by either of them, Burton knew she had another reason to be grateful to Noakes. Newly transferred to CID, she had nursed a hopeless infatuation for the DI. Hopeless, because he had eyes only for Olivia Mullen. She knew now that Noakes must have guessed the lie of the land but – for all he possessed the primitive cunning of a stone age pygmy – he had never held her up to ridicule; had even saved her from making a fool of herself over Markham.

Well, she was older and wiser now. And engaged to a DS in Fraud, thank you very much.

But even now, the sight of the DI's dark head and saturnine good looks, coupled with the melancholy sensitivity which made him somehow unlike any policeman she had ever met, still made her heart miss a beat, so that she became as tongue-tied as any schoolgirl.

She would have to watch herself, Burton thought grimly. Especially around Noakes.

'Sorry, sir, I'm getting ahead of myself.'

'That's all right, Kate.' Markham smiled at her go-getting enthusiasm. Then his face clouded. 'It seems likely Doctor Warr died around the time that he disappeared. Animals and running water took away some of the bones, but most of the skeleton was intact.'

A gruesome abyss opened in Burton's mind, then she veered back to theories.

'D'you think it's connected with the patient abuse scandal at the Newman, sir?'

Before the DI could answer, Noakes weighed in.

'Oh, c'mon. It's a loony bin, right? Any one of the crazies could've done it. Remember when we went there on the St Mary's investigation, Guv ... real *Silence of the Lambs* that was.'

'I remember it all too well, Sergeant.' Markham's tone was trenchant. 'And while we're at it, do you think you could remember that the appropriate designation is special hospital as opposed to "loony bin", and that the inmates are patients rather than "crazies"?'

The DS grinned, not at all abashed by the reproof. 'Righto, Guv.'

Hide of an elephant, thought Burton, wondering for the umpteenth time about the nature of the bond between her uncouth shambling colleague and Markham. Subconsciously, she was jealous of the unspoken understanding she sensed between Noakes and their legendarily chilly boss. Whatever it was, she knew the DS was one of Markham's non-negotiables.

If she had been asked to describe her ideal man, Burton's description would have answered point for point to Gilbert Markham, right down to the far-seeing grey eyes and chiselled refinement quite unlike that of anyone else on the force. Aloof from the petty practices, politics and palpable bids for favour which bedevilled CID, he was the 'sea-green incorruptible' of her ideals. And yet she knew he would never look in her direction. Not in *that* way ...

Burton's mind wandered to Colin, her solid, dependable fiancé. Cupid's dart struck when they worked together on a conspiracy investigation, and before long they were an item. Her parents – particularly her father, who had always been against her joining the police on the grounds that it was 'no job for a woman'– thoroughly approved. If she were totally honest with herself, that was the reason why she'd agreed when Colin suggested they get engaged. That and the thrill of being part of a couple. She need no longer despair of always being the person left behind, seeking a connection, seeking *love*. She would no longer have to wear the armour she had built round herself as a lonely only child. Finally, she could say 'We' not 'I'.

Colin was kind and gentle, with wholesome boy-next-door good looks. He would never let her down. But neither would he ever make her heart skip a beat. Not like Markham with his mysterious air of brooding reserve. The DI was like an iceberg.

You saw just so much, and underneath was the world....

Her feelings for Markham were just a crush, she reminded herself firmly. A schoolgirl crushette on a clever man in authority. Time to suppress her immature hankering and count her blessings. She and Colin made a good team. Love wasn't all hearts and flowers when all was said and done. Noakes was leering as if he could read her thoughts. Burton gave herself a mental shake.

'Hadn't there been threats against Doctor Warr, sir?' She screwed up her face in an effort to remember. 'There was something in the *Gazette* about a woman stabbed to death in Medway Shopping Centre in front of her husband and children... Turned out the attacker was a schizophrenic but Doctor Warr had certified him suitable for care in the community... Didn't the husband start a campaign about it?'

'Oh yeah.' Noakes was interested now. 'I remember that. Name of Hewitt. The husband did a right hatchet job on the Newman. An' not just the doc neither. He had plenty to say about social workers and the rest of the trick cyclists. A right can of worms.'

Burton might have known. Elephants never forget.

'Some of the mud-slinging was unfair,' she interposed. 'I mean, the hospital's got an international reputation for psychotherapy. *The Guardian* did a piece last year about its Freudian research specialists and—'

'Huh ... dirty old men, more like.' Noakes scoffed.

'Of course, it's true that critics said Freud went down deeper, stayed down longer, and came up dirtier than any other psychologist before or since.' Markham smiled thinly. 'But I like to think attitudes have evolved since then.'

It was a brave man who persisted when the DI took that tone but, nothing daunted, Noakes persevered.

'The Newman doesn't have a good name, Guv.' He was clearly rootling through some mental rolodex. 'Scandals down the years an' what not... There were a coupla warders ... er, nurses, whatever you want to call them ... sent down for brutality. An' then there was stuff about hearings being dodgy an' folk being sent there what shouldn't have been.' The DS shook his head ponderously. 'My Muriel said she'd heard all sorts.'

Markham didn't doubt it, Mrs Noakes's capacity for ferreting out discreditable gossip being unmatched in his experience.

Before Noakes could get his second wind, the DI said, 'Actually, Sergeant, the hospital's chequered past represents one line of enquiry.'

The DS looked triumphantly at Burton. The message was clear. Local knowledge trumps namby-pamby sociology bollocks any day of the week.

'Equally,' Markham added, 'we must keep an open mind and follow all lines of enquiry, whether they originate in the community or the hospital's clinical practice.'

Burton kept her face studiously neutral, though inwardly she allowed herself a smirk.

Then she noticed the DI's expression. Something withheld. Her spine prickled. There's more to this than meets the eye, she thought. Noakes clearly felt it too, the big shaggy head cocked to one side as though scenting a change in the wind.

'What I'm about to say doesn't leave this room.' It was the voice of absolute command.

They nodded.

'I was recently tasked with setting up a missing persons investigation.'

Her palms clammy, Burton began to see where this was leading.

'Patients at the Newman seem to have fallen through the

cracks.' The DI's gaze held theirs. 'Individuals who may have been wrongly sectioned or ended up there through systemic failings ... and then disappeared from sight.'

Noakes beat Burton to the punch for once.

'You mean the families might've been in on it with the doctors, Guv ... to get their hands on money or summat?'

Or to get rid of troublesome relatives.

He whistled. 'A conspiracy, like.'

Burton waited, her eyes intent on Markham.

There was something else.

The DI's face was grim.

Suddenly, Burton knew why.

The walls of the office seemed to fall away.

'One of our own,' she whispered.

'Eh?' Noakes was the picture of bewilderment. Then the mist cleared. 'A copper?' he asked incredulously. 'You mean someone from this nick?' His jaw dropped. 'Chuffing Nora.'

'Quite.' Markham's voice was quiet, controlled.

'Why ... I mean, how...?' Burton couldn't take it in.

'There was an anonymous tip-off some time ago to the offices of the *Gazette* claiming that we should check out patients who apparently ended up in the Newman never to be heard of again.'

It sounded like something out of a Hitchcock horror movie.

Markham swiftly got up and closed the door to the outer office before walking across to the window. For a moment, he stood with his back to them, looking sightlessly at the car park.

Then he resumed his seat.

'We know the NHS has its black holes,' he said heavily. 'And some of these cases go back years, to a time when attitudes to mental illness and institutionalized care were very different.'

'But people can't just vanish into thin air.' Burton was

incredulous. 'What about paperwork and procedures?'

Noakes looked at her pityingly.

'Easy to circumvent if you know how,' Markham pointed out.

'Where does a bent copper fit in?' Noakes demanded bluntly.

'Confidential minutes from the patients' council.' Markham's brows contracted. 'They took an unaccountably long time to surface, but eventually came to light as part of the Health Trust's inquiry into mental health tribunals.'

Noakes was struggling to join the dots. 'What's the patients' council, then?'

'It's a totally private forum for patients to air their concerns. No managers allowed. Minutes of meetings strictly confidential. Had it not been for the Trust investigation, it's unlikely anything would've come to light.'

'So, some of 'em in this council thingy said summat about a copper being involved in folk going missing?' Noakes looked sceptical. 'Bit of a long shot, ain't it, Guv?' He received support from an unexpected quarter.

'Could they have been paranoid or fantasizing, sir?' Burton asked before adding carefully, 'I mean, it'd be natural for patients to have a resentment of authority.'

Her colleague had a burst of inspiration. 'An' what about the meds?' he demanded. 'They're probably stuffed full with so many tablets that they're on Planet Zog most of the time.'

'They call it a liquid straitjacket these days,' Burton murmured.

'Yes, that's all perfectly true,' Markham acknowledged levelly. 'Which is why any information from such a source has to be treated with great caution.'

'Did anyone give a name?' Noakes asked shrewdly.

'No.' The DI frowned. 'But they might have been afraid.'

'Yeah.' Noakes warmed to this theme. 'A war – nurse

– might've duffed 'em up … if someone narked or management got wind.'

'Or maybe they worried this officer could get to them,' Burton added. 'But they wanted the information out there somehow.'

It was a sobering thought.

Markham squared his shoulders.

'Right,' he said crisply, 'we'll be running a murder investigation in respect of Doctor Warr, as it's unlikely he ended up in Bromgrove Woods by accident. The autopsy's this afternoon, so we'll know more later today.' He ran a hand impatiently through the thick black hair which curled over the back of his collar. 'Then there's a parallel probe into possible corruption at the Newman and the issue of missing patients.'

The DI looked at Burton.

'Kate, I want you to set up an incident room.'

'At the Newman, sir?'

'Yes. You can take DC Doyle with you. That's if DI Carstairs can spare him from Vice.'

'They've just wrapped up that trafficking case, sir … you know, the one over at the YWCA.'

Markham did know. All too well.

'Excellent, Kate.' He walked her to the door and into the outer office. 'We need PCs, whiteboards, secure telephone. The works. But nothing about the corruption probe to be visible on any displays. There can't be any leaks.'

'Got it.' She hesitated. 'Do you think Doctor Warr's death and the mispers are linked, sir?'

'My personal feeling is that there's a connection, yes.' He smiled down at her. 'You know I don't like coincidences.'

Then the door to the DI's room clicked shut behind her.

For a moment, she stood irresolute, wistfully looking back

at her colleagues through the vertical blinds which screened the glass partition walls. The DS was happily playing with the steel balance balls on a pendulum relaxation toy which sat on Markham's desk, setting them in motion with the gleeful absorption of a child.

She felt a sudden sharp pang, envying their complicity with a fierceness which took her by surprise. She wanted to make friends but didn't know how.

Why can't I be as relaxed as that around the boss? Why am I so uptight? Why doesn't he let his guard down with me the way he does with Noakes?

The boss was so reclusive, yet he had let George Noakes into his life. Could he ever be as comfortable with her?

Oh, for God's sake, she told herself. There's an incident room to get sorted and here I am mooning around like a soppy adolescent. Get a grip, Burton! Purposefully, she headed towards the door.

'Have you quite finished playing with that thing?' Markham asked the DS, but his tone was indulgent.

Reluctantly, Noakes turned his attention away from the gadget.

'Champion,' he said. 'Think I'll get one of those for our Nat's birthday.'

The DI thought it infinitely more likely that Noakes's perma-tanned daughter, the undisputed doyenne of Bromgrove's nightclubs, would prefer a pair of Jimmy Choos, but kept his opinion to himself. Let the doting father cherish his illusions.

'So.' Noakes looked beadily at his boss. 'Who's the weak link?' Then, holding up a stubby forefinger gnomically, he volunteered the surprising intelligence, 'Ackshually, I might have an idea about that.'

Markham waited.

'My Muriel went to the Newman Open Day last year,' Noakes said at last. 'With the Women's Guild.' He wrinkled his nose. 'Didn't fancy it meself. Places like that give me the heebie jeebies.'

He gave a pleasurable shudder then continued. 'The gold braid mob was out in force along of all the local big wigs. DCI Sidney an' all them.'

He looked closely at Markham.

'The Chief Super was there an' all.'

The DI didn't move a muscle, though a pulse had begun hammering near his jaw.

'The missus said he looked like he owned the place.'

A pause.

'Really at home.'

Another pause then, 'Too much at home.'

Too much at home.

Such a small deadly phrase.

And Muriel Noakes – bossy, overbearing, bumptious – had registered that false note.

Noakes held his boss's eyes.

'It's Chief Superintendent Rees, isn't it, Guv?'

The DI nodded.

Chief Superintendent Philip Rees.

Gold Commander on the case.

After Noakes had padded away on various unspecified errands (no doubt involving a detour by way of the canteen), Markham remained at his desk, his mind travelling to the previous week's meeting with DCC George Ashton....

Ruddy cheeked and stocky, with a fine head of iron-grey hair, Ashton looked more like a ploughman than second in command of Bromgrove's finest. But the DI knew better than to underestimate 'Farmer George', fully aware of the shrewd intelligence concealed behind that bluff exterior. He would have to tread carefully. If this blew up at some future date, or a trial imploded for want of 'due process', the DI had no doubt his superiors would throw him to the wolves without a second thought.

'Is the investigation into Chief Superintendent Rees official, sir? I mean, shouldn't Professional Standards be involved?'

Markham could see the question was unwelcome, but Ashton met his gaze squarely.

'You can take it the investigation is authorized at the highest level, Inspector.' He allowed a pause for this to sink in. 'But given the sensitive context – special hospital, vulnerable adults and so forth – you will report directly to me.'

The DCC's face was open and guileless, his tone avuncular. 'Don't look so worried, man. Baseless accusations against senior officers are an occupational hazard.'

Markham found this less than reassuring, but knew better than to push his luck. Ashton had clearly brought down the portcullis on any further discussion of Rees.

'Concentrate on these missing patients at the Newman, Inspector. And keep all briefings "need to know". With the *Gazette* and these campaigners sniffing around ... well, let's just say I don't want to hear rumours of another Shipman.'

'Understood, sir.'

Less than a week later, Markham learned that his SIO on the Newman investigation was none other than Chief Superintendent Philip Rees.

Well, he reasoned, the Chief Super hadn't been suspended or stripped of his rank. And gold command was more about honour and glory than anything else – grandly remote and 'hands off' rather than getting stuck in with the troops – so he could be kept out of the team's direct orbit.

On reflection, it would have been more likely to raise eyebrows if Rees *hadn't* received the appointment. And yet, Markham was uneasy, still in the dark as to the DCC's cunning plan – if indeed there *was* a plan as opposed to its being business as usual....

What Noakes termed arse-covering was clearly the order of the day. Wearily, Markham booted up his computer and prepared to compose an e mail. Time to get the DCC's *imprimatur* in writing.

And then off to the scene of the crime.

2

Through the Looking Glass

THE NEWMAN HOSPITAL, SITUATED behind Bromgrove General on
the outskirts of the town in the quiet suburb of Medway, was
a disconcerting conglomeration of redbrick gothic architecture
and twenty-first century modernism.

The Victorian clocktower which dominated the forecourt –
once part of the old workhouse – was flanked on either side by
low gunmetal grey extensions which put Markham in mind of
U-boats.

As they lingered at the front of the building in the rapidly
cooling Monday afternoon air, it was clear Noakes didn't much
care for his surroundings.

'Why'd they bother with all them daft slogans?' He jabbed
a finger at various hoardings bearing multi-coloured mottoes:
With You On The Journey and By Your Side. 'Do they think
folk won't notice it's a nut house?'

'Mental health facility,' the DI corrected resignedly. Short of
a personality transplant, there was precious little prospect of
Noakes behaving in a manner that could remotely be described
as PC. The best Markham could hope for was that he and Kate

Burton would be able to absorb the worst of it.

'An' what's that load of old junk?' A pudgy digit stabbed the air again.

Following the direction of Noakes's gaze, Markham saw what appeared to be a collection of suitcases and rucksacks cast in concrete next to some granite blocks bearing the imprint of footsteps.

'I would imagine it's an art installation,' he observed mildly. 'On the theme of journeys … Yes,' he bent down to look at the small plaque at its base, 'it's entitled Voyage of Recovery.'

'Oh, I'm sure that makes the psychos feel a whole lot better,' opined his companion with heavy sarcasm. 'Yeah, cop a load of that an' no need for the old hypodermics.'

'Stow it, Sergeant,' Markham rapped, 'or I'll think seriously about recommending you for diversity awareness training. And for God's sake watch your language. The people here are patients or service users, got it?'

A grunt was all the response he got.

Although the reception and waiting area – located to the left of the clock tower – occupied a double height atrium flooded with light, Markham had the unpleasant sensation of being in some sort of air lock, as though all the oxygen had been sucked out. The U-boat analogy again.

Swivelling CCTV and red lights winking heightened the feeling of deadening claustrophobia in this universe which had to have eyes wide open twenty-four hours a day. Markham felt his own pupils begin to throb in sympathy.

By his side, Noakes shuffled from one foot to the other, casting those furtive glances with which he was wont to approach situations outside the norm.

A pretty blonde receptionist with a smile of unnatural brilliance greeted them at the glass-walled central island in the entrance foyer. Having issued the two men with ID badges, she kept up a non-stop stream of patter while whisking them at dizzying speed through the building, four inch stilettos notwithstanding.

'I'm Hayley Macdonald. Our managing director – Ms Holder – thought you might like a quick tour, jus' so you know the layout.'

Markham forbore to mention that this was not his first visit to the Newman.

'All the wards are colour coded and named after famous rivers. Nile, Danube, Volga, Thames and Rhine.'

Noakes opened his mouth but, at a look from Markham, shut it again.

'They're all single sex. Rhine's the intensive care secure unit for service users on a section or in long-term treatment.'

Flashing through the complex like a chirruping kingfisher, Hayley gestured right and left.

'All the corridors have light tubes and skylights.'

'Why's that, luv?' Noakes couldn't resist.

'Therapeutic,' she replied with the air of one who knew her script and was sticking to it. 'Helps to promote mindfulness and wellbeing innit. They c'n look at the clouds and things.' She paused at one of the floor-to-ceiling French windows. 'We've got garden spaces too. Bringing the outdoors indoors.'

'Like a bit of hoeing do they, luv?'

Hayley looked slightly flustered.

'Well, there's safety to think about.'

'Of course.'

Markham shot another meaningful look at the DS.

It was clear the one-storey facility extended a long way back.

'There's eighty beds in the main wards. All en suite.' Poignantly, Hayley's voice held a note of proprietorial pride.

'Then we've got twenty beds in the critical care section. Music and art studios are round the back of the clock tower, an' here's a multi faith room where you c'n jus' chill.' She whipped open the door to a small room, one wall of which comprised a stained glass window where a gaily coloured boat headed across choppy turquoise seas to a lighthouse painted in vertical red and white stripes like a fairground helter skelter.

'Very calming,' Markham declared firmly before Noakes could say anything untoward. Hayley beamed at him. 'I sit here myself sometimes,' she confided, 'if I want a bit of peace and quiet.'

Then they were off again. They passed what seemed like acres of glass and brightly-coloured day lounges ('break out spaces,' Hayley pronounced, with no apparent sense of irony) before arriving at a set of double doors next to which was a sign marked Forensic. Through the doors, Markham glimpsed the metal detector arch and plexiglass reinforced nursing station.

Hayley was palpably ill at ease now. 'This is the secure area,' she said uncomfortably. 'Ms Holder said I should leave this bit to her.'

'Sure,' Markham said easily, frowning at Noakes who was boggling at the interior of the ward as though expecting Nurse Ratched to emerge at any moment.

Visibly relieved, Hayley seemed to recover her sang-froid. 'P'raps you'd like to see our shop,' she suggested. 'There's a little café too.'

Noakes rubbed his hands. 'Now you're talking my language, luv.'

At that moment, a kindly faced individual who looked to be in his early sixties emerged through a side door pushing a trolley stacked with boxes and packages of various shapes and sizes.

''Lo, Ernie,' Hayley greeted him cheerfully. Then to her visitors, 'This is Ernie Roberts, our head porter.'

Markham recognized the name of the man who'd discovered the skeleton in Bromgrove Woods.

Mr Roberts ducked his head in acknowledgement and smiled shyly at the young receptionist with whom he was clearly something of a favourite.

'I'm jus' taking these, er, visitors, to the caff.'

'Another half hour till my break, young Hayley.' It was a gentle voice with a soft burr.

Markham was surprised to find Mr Roberts back at work after the shock he'd had. But he could tell the man was old school. Used to soldiering on.

'See ya then.' Hayley waved as her colleague disappeared down the corridor.

'He's lovely is Ernie,' she told them. 'A real sweetheart. Lost his wife a while back an' lives on his own. I dog-sit for him sometimes.'

Momentarily, Noakes was distracted from thoughts of food.

'What's those?' he asked, pointing to a framed photograph hanging on the wall opposite, which must originally have been black and white but was now faded to sepia, giving it a ghostly look.

Markham moved alongside him to look. After a brief hesitation, Hayley joined them.

The photograph appeared to show little clapboard garden pavilions dotted across a sandy expanse like hives.

That was all. Nothing else.

Noakes was almost nose to nose with the glass.

'There's a signature or summat in the right-hand corner,' he said. 'Yeah ... *Your Friend* ... that's what it says.'

He straightened up and grinned at Hayley who was once

more looking flustered.

'Spooky, that. Got yourself a poltergeist or summat?'

'Oh, I think that prob'ly just means the Friends of the Newman, Mr Noakes. A gift from the volunteers, y'see.' With a flash of inspiration, she added, 'They raise funds to send patients on trips ... holiday chalets ... stuff like that.'

The DS let it go and wandered off to look at a startling seaside mural – more boats bobbing up and down in a garish marina – with Hayley hovering at his elbow like an anxious gallery assistant.

Markham, meanwhile, stood lost in thought in front of the strange photograph.

Your Friend.

Suddenly, he realized where he had seen those words before.

At school. A history book about the Russian Revolution. There was a sinister monk called Rasputin, with a long beard and piercing eyes, whose evil influence brought down the royal family and led to their death by firing squad. A hypnotist and fraudster ... That was how he signed off letters to his victims. *Your Friend.*

Despite the airless warmth of the corridor, Markham shivered. It was a disquieting association. Almost a warning. Was there an evil genius lying in wait somewhere in this strange sealed-off world?

He looked again at the faded photograph, so incongruous next to the relentlessly upbeat artwork surrounding it. Those little chalets, or whatever they were, struck a chill in their desolate isolation. No-one can hear you scream, he thought.

Hayley was looking askance at Noakes. Oh God, better get in there before he outraged her sensibilities past all hope of redemption.

Crisis averted. 'They've got Wagon Wheels in the caff,' she

said cunningly.

As by a Pavlovian reflex, the DS docilely aborted his commentary on the deficiencies of institutional modern art. 'You up for a cuppa, Guv?' he said over his shoulder.

Markham resigned himself to the inevitable and followed the pair back along the corridor. Behind him, there was the faint hydraulic hiss of a swing door, but when he turned around there was no-one there. That was the thing about this hermetically-secured universe, he reflected. Like an aquarium, it somehow deadened sound and muffled ordinary human noises so that they seemed to come from a long way away ...

The other two were looking at him. 'Lead on, Hayley,' he said politely.

Markham felt better once they were seated in the café where they had the place to themselves. The coffee was surprisingly good and the Wagon Wheels restored Noakes's good humour, while the seating area was light and airy with a pleasant view onto a landscaped patio bright with catkins and primroses. A motherly looking woman greeted Hayley cheerfully before bustling off to do some stock-taking.

'Linda Harelock's our longest-serving befriender,' the receptionist explained.

Noakes looked startled. 'What's one of them then, luv?' he mumbled through a mouthful of biscuit, looking round warily as though he anticipated a laying on of hands.

Hayley giggled at the expression on his face.

'Oh, that jus' means the volunteers – folk who help with the café and mobile library. They visit patients too, like if they don't have any family or friends.'

Noakes relaxed again, but Markham noticed he was back to

the furtive glances.

Hayley noticed too.

'The patients have their own dining areas on the wards,' she said casually. 'This is mainly for visitors.'

Markham was conscious of relief that the evil hour for inducting his sergeant into appropriate behaviour around service users was not yet upon them.

'What's in the old part of the building?' he enquired.

'Oh, that's the archives, where they keep all the records. Lin and the befrienders help out in there sometimes.' Surreptitiously, Hayley slipped off her stilettos under the table, enjoying the sensation of cool linoleum against her soles. 'The Research Centre's in there too, plus some therapy rooms.'

'Looks a bit gloomy,' put in Noakes. 'Like Broadmoor or one of them places.'

'That's all changing, Mr Noakes,' Hayley said solemnly. 'They're redesigning all the old hospitals ... gonna be miles cheerier ... eco-friendly an' everything.'

The DI looked at her earnest little face.

Cosmetic rebranding, he thought, but the same demons seething beneath.

Suddenly, Hayley stiffened. A petite woman with an olive complexion and long dark hair coiled into a chignon at the nape of her neck was threading her way through the tables towards them. Her entire appearance was an exemplar of executive power dressing, while long blood-red fingernails put Markham in mind of a bird of prey.

'Thank you, Hayley.' It was a husky contralto. 'I'll take it from here.'

Dismissed, the receptionist scrabbled for her shoes. Markham smiled warmly at her. 'Thank you for taking care of us, Hayley,' he said.

'Nice lass that.' Noakes eyed her retreating figure with avuncular benevolence, oblivious of the impatience which vibrated through every inch of the Pocket Venus at his side.

'Quite,' was the crisp response. 'Now, if we could get on.'

The two men stood and introductions were duly made before Ms Holder ushered them along several more corridors to her office.

'Bit quiet, isn't it?' said Noakes to no-one in particular.

'You won't see much of our service users in the administrative section of the building. Not from any lack of transparency.' She bestowed a chilly smile on Noakes. 'It's simply that the wards are pretty much self-contained, so there's no reason for them to go further afield.'

'Very cosy, I'm sure,' came the reply.

The director looked hard at him, as though probing the observation for any trace of sarcasm, but the DS's expression of sunny innocence was inscrutable. Clearly concluding that he was an amiable simpleton, their guide opened the door to her sanctum.

Claire Holder's huge office was impressive. Parquet wood flooring with what, to Markham's eye, looked very much like an Aubusson carpet in filigree blue and ivory. Two comfortable wingback armchairs, whose aquamarine needlepoint upholstery picked up the delicate tints of the carpet, were positioned either side of a glass coffee table bearing copies of Country Life. A large walnut Partners desk stood in front of bay French windows, framed by navy swag curtains, which gave access to what looked like a private walled garden. A door to the right of the desk was half-open, and Markham caught a glimpse of a luxuriously appointed private bathroom before the director hastily shut it. One side of the room held an oval conference table and chairs, while the other featured a mahogany sideboard with state-of-the-art coffee maker and fine bone china. A glorious floral arrangement – hellebore and winter jasmine – stood in a blue and white porcelain jardinière next to the window, echoing the room's colour palette. The air was overlaid with a subtle fragrance, as of cinnamon and cloves.

A sardonic comment on these plush surroundings gleamed in Noakes's eye.

Nice work if you can get it!

Imperceptibly, Markham shook his head to forestall any impertinent observation, not however without the rueful reflection that Claire Holder's quarters would give their Chief Super a run for his money.

With an imperious gesture, the director waved them to be seated and settled herself behind the desk.

With the light behind her, Markham could now see that the woman was not as composed as she had at first appeared. Despite heavy make-up, her dark eyes looked bloodshot and the manicured hands which rested on her desk's leather blotter were trembling. Following the direction of the DI's gaze, she moved them to her lap.

'Your colleague Sergeant Burton is setting up an incident room for you next to the archives room in the clock building. It should satisfy your requirements, but please don't hesitate to tell me if there is anything else you need. I would appreciate it if you could ensure as little interference with the hospital's day-to-day routines as possible.'

Maximum efficiency, minimum warmth.

'This is a murder inquiry, Ms Holder, and everything else is subordinate to that.' The DI felt an instinctive antipathy to this beautifully groomed woman whose smile did not reach her eyes, but he sought to hide it. With a steely glance at Noakes, he reassured her, 'We will of course at all times respect the patients' dignity and privacy.'

'Thank you, Inspector.' She patted her immaculate chignon and flicked an invisible speck off the lapel of her soft wool jacket. A discreet glance at the ormolu clock on her desk suggested that her mind was elsewhere. Committee meetings and action plans, Markham surmised wryly.

'Will you be wanting to start interviews today?' she asked. That was good. Such pragmatism at least made a change from the usual bill of fare on such occasions: the simulated outrage ('You can't seriously be suggesting ...'), followed by grudging compliance ('Well, of course we've got nothing to hide ...'), accompanied by lashings of insincerity to appease affronted executive egos ('Just a matter of routine ... purposes of elimination' etcetera).

'I'd like to get started on those first thing tomorrow morning,' the DI answered smoothly, 'but if you felt able to spare us a few minutes of your time now ...'

He could tell the suggestion was unwelcome, but she answered steadily enough, 'Of course.' A muscle leaped at the corner of her carefully lipsticked mouth. 'I understand you've been able to make an identification ...'

'Yes. The deceased is Doctor Jonathan Warr, one of your consultants who went missing early last year.' No point in sugar coating it. 'We believe he was murdered, but will know more after the autopsy.'

She had herself well under control now. Just that tell-tale tic hinting at turmoil behind the veneer.

'It was a shock to everyone when Jon didn't turn up to work. We'd been at the Mental Health Conference at the Wellcome Institute in London together only the day before.'

'Jus' the two of you?' Noakes wore an expression of Confucian impenetrability as though to preserve himself from any suspicion of salaciousness.

'That's right.' There was a flush of angry colour on the sallow cheeks, but she didn't rise to the bait. Markham felt a certain reluctant admiration begin to stir.

'What was your impression of his state of mind?'

'Well, there were problems with his wife Deirdre.' Her voice hardened. 'And he was terribly upset by the patient abuse inquiry... I'd never seen him so depressed.' The black eyes suddenly flashed fire. 'He was a wonderful, caring man, absolutely devoted to his patients. It was scandalous the way those campaigners persecuted him.'

'Sounds like he had a friend in you, luv,' Noakes observed insinuatingly.

'He was my professional mentor,' the director replied with calm dignity.

That and what else besides, wondered Markham. Was this a case of an illicit relationship gone sour? Had Warr refused to leave his wife for her? Or were the two of them up to something which went awry? Fraud? Malpractice? Something darker?

Markham rose to his feet, sensing they would get nothing further out of her at this juncture.

He intercepted a glance at the small top drawer of her desk. Drawer with a key. A pound to a penny Claire Holder had a bottle of something stashed away in there. Gin. Vodka. Whisky. From the look on her face, she needed that drink badly ...

It was a relief to get outside and gulp down lungfuls of cold air. Even the gathering twilight was welcome. Markham felt oddly disorientated. As though, like Alice, he had passed through the looking glass. Well, now he was back on the right side again.

'Like Antiques Roadshow in that office,' Noakes offered

sourly. 'An' what's the betting her nibs is necking it down before we're even out of the car park?'

'Yes, I'd say the mini bar is well and truly open,' the DI agreed.

Noakes gave a convulsive shudder. 'That place creeps me out, Guv. All shiny and nicey-nicey, but not real if you get me.'

Markham did.

'I want to pay a call on those campaigners Ms Holder mentioned.'

'Oh yeah?'

'They've got an office round the corner, above Age Concern in the shopping centre.' The DI looked over his shoulder at the hospital, its extensions seeming more submarine-like than ever in the misty evening air. 'We can swing by here later to check in with Burton and Doyle.'

With that, the two men walked off towards their car.

Claire Holder sat on the edge of the loo in her private bath-room, the door locked, fortifying herself exactly as Markham had envisaged.

Just one drink, she told herself. Just one drink.

And by God she needed it.

That inspector was a handsome devil. Reminded her of Jon before …

Hastily, she took another swig.

Careful now. She had a meeting with the Trustees in fifteen minutes. Wouldn't do to let all those awful Colonel Blimps catch a whiff of Stolichnaya Premium brand. Where the fuck were those double-strength mints?

The awful lecherous look on that buffoon-like sergeant's face. God.

It wasn't like that with Jon. It wasn't gross or crude. She

believed in him. Believed that together they served a higher purpose. And then it all went wrong.

Enough of this. With shaking hands, she smoothed down her skirt and meticulously began to reapply her makeup.

Perfect. And no alcohol breath.

She was ready for business.

3

Sleep No More

TWILIGHT WAS DRAWING IN as Markham and Noakes approached Age Concern in the Medway shopping centre, the street lamps' milky phosphorescence leaching daylight from the evening sky. Yet both men were glad to be away from the Newman Hospital with its relentless, wide awake watchfulness.

The centre was in fact little more than two covered arcades for the big name retailers – WHSmith, Marks and Spencer, Boots and the like – with a dreary little street in between, where Poundland and charity shops jostled for custom.

Age Concern was halfway down this unprepossessing row. A doorway to the right of the shop bore a buzzer with the intercom discreetly labelled Behind Closed Doors. Markham pressed the button and the door clicked open. They climbed a flight of dark, rank-smelling stairs, emerging onto a narrow landing with two more doors.

A pale ginger-haired man with a straggly Karl Marx beard suddenly appeared before them in his shirtsleeves. Squinting uncertainly at them in the gloom, he said, 'That was speedy. I wasn't expecting you guys till tomorrow.'

Following him into a cramped office overlooking the street, they were confronted with an industrial size photocopier which had clearly ground to a halt mid-cycle, the machine's inky entrails exposed to view and stacks of leaflets dotting the sludge-coloured rattan carpet.

'Sorry to disappoint you, sir.' The DI grimaced sympathetically while Noakes took in the dispiriting décor of faded floral wallpaper, limp moss-green curtains hanging at a drunken angle, and grubby formica table overflowing with takeaway cartons. It was the kind of place his missus would say should carry a warning to wipe your feet on the way out. 'I gather you're expecting a repair service,' Markham continued. 'In fact, we're here on another matter entirely.'

Introductions were made, their softly-spoken interlocutor explaining that he was David Belcher, lead (and doubtless sole) coordinator of the Behind Closed Doors campaign, before inviting them to take a seat. Perched gingerly on the edge of an incongruously chintzy sofa, Noakes averted his eyes from various stains and blotches which suggested it hadn't been cleaned in decades. God, he thought, let's get out of bleeding Botulism Central before we catch summat.

Markham showed not the slightest sign of discomfort, as much at his ease in the comfortless garret as if taking tea with the Queen. You had to hand it to the guvnor, the DS reflected with grudging admiration, he treated everyone alike. Didn't matter if they were the Deputy Chief Constable or a dustman, it was all the same to him.

The DI's grave courtesy had its effect on the other whose offer of refreshments was (with an inward shudder on Noakes's part) declined. Coiling his lanky frame into a grungy armchair opposite them, Belcher apologized for the chaos. 'We run this place on a shoestring, and everything's at sixes and sevens today.'

'You're in the middle of a mailshot, I see. Admirable work, acting as a watchdog for patients' rights.' Markham paused. 'Hopefully the mental health landscape's changed for the better thanks to the Blom-Cooper and Boynton inquiries,' he added with an encouraging smile.

'Maybe in places like Ashworth and Rampton, Inspector. But the trendy brigade's moved on now. The Newman doesn't attract many column inches these days.'

'But surely the current investigation's a positive development.'

'D'you know how long it took to get that off the ground, Inspector?' David Belcher's hands were clenched as though he badly wanted to punch someone. 'Years. And we were stone-walled all the way.' He took a ragged breath. 'If it hadn't been for those lowlife nurses getting sent down, the Newman's man-agers would've got away with it. Just tap-danced their way out of trouble.' A hand came up to tug the straggly beard. 'But after that, well, the Trust couldn't look the other way.'

The DS eyed him shrewdly. 'Know someone in there do you, mate? A patient?'

Belcher looked at Noakes's face. Whatever he saw there seemed to reassure him.

'Yeah, my brother Mikey.' Another tug of the beard. 'Personality disorder. Our shitty childhood may have had some-thing to do with it ...'

'At least he's got you in his corner.'

'Violent sociopath. That's what they called him. But he was never violent with me.'

'Any chance they'll let him out one day?' Noakes's voice was surprisingly gentle.

'Oh, they've marked him down as a troublemaker, Sergeant. He's on the patients' council, you see.'

'Don't they like 'em to have a bit of a say, then?'

A strange, almost shifty expression crossed Belcher's face.

'Not it if means opening a can of worms.'

'Can of worms?' Markham leaned forward intently.

'Stories from old-timers ... about more than just abuse.' Belcher gave an embarrassed laugh. 'Look, I know this sounds far-fetched ... like something out of *Shutter Island* ... but Mikey was freaked out.' The hazel eyes held a desperate appeal. 'Word was that people had disappeared and one of your lot was involved.' He swallowed hard, prominent Adam's apple painfully visible under the transparent skin. 'There must've been something in it, cos they suspended my visits after that. Oh, sure, they dressed it up with a load of bollocks about patient protocols and change of medication, but the bottom line was I didn't get to see him.'

'Rest assured, we'll be looking into that, Mr Belcher,' Markham said seriously. The room was very quiet, the sound of creaking grilles in the street below signalling the end of the working day.

'You may be aware that a body was discovered in Bromgrove Woods.'

'Yes, I had heard, Inspector.'

'Doctor Jonathan Warr from the Newman. We believe him to have been murdered.'

Again, a long convulsive swallow and a flush that ran up under the dead white complexion like an angry rash.

'I won't pretend to be sorry, Inspector. I'm not that much of a hypocrite.' Belcher's voice was hoarse with suppressed emotion.

Markham waited. It was one of his gifts, the capacity to refrain from filling a silence.

'He was an arrogant piece of work. One of those doctors with a God complex.' Belcher made a self-deprecating gesture.

'Look, I don't have a chip. Never made it to university myself ...
lost several years to drink and drugs ... But I know a phoney
when I see one.' He shook his head slowly. 'Oh sure, Warr had
a string of initials after his name and all the bigwigs eating
out of his hand. But he was managing Mikey's case all wrong
... experimenting on him with way-out treatments or some
such, cos Mikey was doing really well, then once Warr came
along he went a bit haywire.'

'Could what your Mikey said about folk disappearing be
down to his mental problems?' Noakes asked. 'Or maybe,'
the DS screwed up his bulldog features in a comically touching effort to telegraph sympathy, 'there was hallucinations or
summat that stopped him thinking straight ... voices from the
radio an' all that.'

'Anything's possible, Sergeant. But I think Mikey was
proper scared ... cowed almost. I'd never seen him like that
before.'

Belcher looked straight at Markham.

'Something was wrong at that hospital, Inspector. And I
think Doctor Warr and that harpy girlfriend of his were both
in on it.'

He sighed and gestured to the photocopier. 'This is a tinpot
– some would say crackpot – outfit. But at least we're raising
awareness.'

The DS scooped up a handful of leaflets. He cleared his
throat. 'Good on you, mate.' Without looking at Markham, he
added, 'We'll have a few of these for the station.'

The DI raised a quizzical eyebrow. Wonders would never
cease. Noakes'd be suggesting a group hug next. 'We can see
ourselves out, Mr Belcher,' he said cordially. 'No need for you to
come downstairs.'

It was quite dark now, with only a few idlers here and there.

A heavy silence seemed to press in on them, strangely and suddenly hushing the lonely little precinct.

'Poor bugger,' Noakes said unexpectedly as they made their way back to Medway car park. 'Some folk jus' never catch a break.'

Markham too felt compassion for Belcher stealing over his heart. But he knew better than to be mastered by first impressions. He recalled the campaigner's sinewy whipcord arms and the stealthy vigilance of his expression – like that of a cornered animal. The man had been frank about his hatred of Doctor Warr. But that could have been the double bluff of a diseased mind ... And what about the sociopathic Mikey? Could he be pulling strings from inside the Newman?

Noakes had stopped under a street lamp and was scrutinizing one of the poorly printed leaflets.

'Seems like Belcher had teamed up with that bloke Hewitt, Guv. Y'know, the one whose wife died cos Warr screwed up.' He peered closely at the grainy type. 'They wanted Warr's balls on a plate.'

'In which case, they got more than they bargained for,' Markham said curtly, thinking of the pitiful skeletal remains unearthed in Bromgrove Woods and the SOCOs in their white decontamination suits.

Noakes had the grace to look embarrassed.

'Sorry, boss, no disrespect intended.'

The DI sighed. 'It's all right, Noakesy.' Under the light, his face looked suddenly haggard. 'I can't help feeling there's something particularly twisted about this one ... the way Doctor Warr was just dumped and left to rot. Bones, teeth, dental records. The ultimate indignity. Whatever the man's professional failings – he didn't deserve that. His family didn't deserve that.'

Noakes stuffed the wodge of leaflets into his jacket pockets. 'What d'you think Belcher meant about Warr's girlfriend?'

'Hmmm. He said they were both in on it, whatever "it" meant.' Markham thought back to the opulence of Claire Holder's office. 'A financial scam of some sort ... a revenue stream that didn't bear close scrutiny. Or something worse ... clinical malpractice.' Wearily, he pinched the bridge of his nose. 'Intimidation of patients seems the least of it.'

They had reached the car park.

'Where to now, Guv?'

'Let's check in with Burton and then we'll call it a day.'

At that moment, Markham's mobile rang.

The call was over in a matter of seconds.

'Results of the autopsy on Doctor Warr. Fracture of the hyoid confirming strangulation.' The DI's face wore a puzzled expression. 'There was something else too. A transorbital wound.'

'Eh?'

'Doctor Warr had been stabbed through the eye, most likely post mortem.'

The DS looked baffled. 'Why do that?' Then his expression cleared. 'Maybe it was part of some sicko ritual, Guv. Satanic, summat like that.'

'"Eyes are the windows to the soul."' Markham spoke as though to himself. 'By mutilating Doctor Warr's eyes, maybe the killer was trying to send a message that he was evil.'

Noakes looked dubious. 'Or maybe he just got his jollies doing a spot of slice an' dice.'

'This puts a new complexion on things, Sergeant.' Markham's lean frame was taut with urgency. 'We've got a seriously disturbed killer on our hands.'

'One of the loo – er, patients, from the hospital, boss?'

'We'll need to check discharges and visitor records for the period before Doctor Warr went missing.' The DI was thoughtful. 'We could be looking at a former or current patient with a grudge against Doctor Warr. If current, then he or she could be playing someone on the outside.'

Noakes lowered his voice. 'Where does Chief Superintendent Rees fit into this?'

'I wish I knew, Sergeant.' Markham's gaze was steady on the other's face. 'Maybe there's no link between the patient disappearances and Doctor Warr's death ... though all my instincts tell me otherwise.'

Suddenly, he remembered the strange picture inscribed with the words *Your Friend*.

Were mutilator and mystery photographer one and the same?

Had a secret from the past led to murder in the present?

Was their killer mad or bad? Maniac or master manipulator?

Despite the cold night air, he felt feverishly light-headed, as though his head might explode with unanswered questions.

'C'mon, boss.' Noakes said phlegmatically, opening the car door. 'Knowing Burton, she'll have it all mapped out on those ruddy flow charts she's so fond of. An' there was this poncey shrink manual she was rabbiting on about. Sounded like S & M for Beginners or some crap like that.'

Despite his exhaustion, the DI's lips twitched.

'I think you'll find she was referring to the *Diagnostic and Statistical Manual of Mental Disorders*, Sergeant. Currently in its fifth edition. DSM for short.'

'Yeah, well, I reminded her it's a blooming police station, not Pervs 'R' Us. What the chuffing hell she thinks we're going to learn from garbage like that is anybody's guess....'

Markham could only hope and pray Burton didn't move on

to *Krafft-Ebing*. George Noakes's likely reaction to the murkier reaches of the Psychopathia Sexualis was something he didn't care to witness.

In the gloaming, Medway was deserted now, the only sign of life a dim silhouette at the window above Age Concern where David Belcher stood forlornly lost in his own thoughts.

As Noakes had feared, Kate Burton was immersed in spreadsheets and flow charts when they arrived at the improvised incident room in the clock building. A pile of what looked like psychology textbooks and the dreaded DSM were at her feet.

DC Doyle – a gangling redhead whose slick dress sense belied his fresh farm boy looks – greeted them enthusiastically. Judging from the look he exchanged with Noakes, the young detective had reached saturation point when it came to psychological theorizing.

'Seen any fruit and nuts yet, mate?' Noakes asked jocularly.

Burton frowned.

'I mean service users,' he amended, with a shrug that spoke volumes.

'They gave us a tour of the wards,' Doyle answered, his tone constrained. 'Seemed peaceful enough. The odd shuffling dead-eyed character, but what else did you expect in a mental hospital?'

Markham glanced round from his inventory of the room.

'Took you round the secure area as well, did they?'

'Not as such, sir.' Doyle was apologetic. 'We just peeked through the doors.' He looked anxiously at the DI. 'There was a ward round, see ...'

'No problem,' Markham replied smoothly, inwardly resolving to gain access to patients on that ward before the investigation was very much older.

'It's all state of the art,' Burton said happily. 'Everything biometric and eco-friendly. The patients have had a lot of input apparently.'

She seemed perfectly at ease. Fresh from an MA in Gender and Modern Policing – via her sabbatical year at Bromgrove University – the case represented a sociological puzzle the DS was keen to unlock.

Markham wished he shared her certainty.

The adjoining archives room was the usual musty amalgam of mobile shelving, rolling stacks and old-fashioned index card cabinets. The mere sight of its polyglot layout gave the DI a throbbing pain in the temples. And yet, for all he knew, this unprepossessing space might hold the key to Doctor Warr's murder and abuses going back years ...

Suddenly, there was a violent rattling and they all jumped. Through the long oblong side window which looked out onto a narrow path running between old and new buildings, Markham saw rain pouring down like a cataract. The elemental disturbance felt somehow appropriate.

Noakes yawned ostentatiously. Burton, on the other hand, was conspicuously bright-eyed and bushy-tailed. Just like the freaking Duracell Bunny, he thought disgustedly. Well, he'd had enough for one day. The guvnor too by the looks of it. Burton would get started on symptoms and syndromes, or some other highfalutin malarkey, unless he stepped in sharpish.

'You up for a pint, Guv?'

The dark eyes were grateful.

'Not tonight, Noakesy. I need to check in with Dimples.' As Doctor Doug Davidson the police pathologist was irreverently known.

'Game plan for tomorrow, sir?' Doyle clearly thought it politic to enquire.

'I want you and Kate checking records for discharges and visits for the last eighteen months.' It was the kind of methodical grunt work at which Burton excelled, though Doyle looked less than enthralled by the prospect.

'What will you and Noakes be doing, sir?' asked Burton jealously.

'Visiting the *Gazette*'s offices for a word with whoever's covering the missing patients story.'

'Pete Darlington,' grunted Noakes. 'He's a slippery customer an' no mistake.'

'After that, I want to speak to Ted Cartwright down at the council.'

'Isn't he the one who nearly got struck off?' asked Doyle with a flare of interest.

'The very same,' Markham confirmed grimly.

'Oh yeah.' Noakes looked as though there was a bad smell under his nose. 'Nasty piece of work. Finger in every pie an' sly like you wouldn't believe. Nearly got those psycho warders off.'

'Nurses,' Markham and Burton said in unison.

'Living it large for a legal aid merchant,' the DS continued ruminatively. 'I mean ter say, how'd he come by that whopping great barn of his? Like summat out of *Hello* or one of them fancy magazines. My Muriel—'

Mrs Noakes's views on Bromgrove's kleptocracy being only too familiar, Markham hastily cut in.

'As you say, Sergeant, a shady character who I think repays closer examination.' Markham gazed out into the watery darkness. 'We need to get started on staff interviews here tomorrow as well. And I want to recce the Forensic unit.' He nodded significantly at Noakes. 'Get the lie of the land. Take a look at Mikey Belcher.' Succinctly, he briefed the other two on his visit to Behind Closed Doors and the post-mortem mutilation of Doctor Warr's body. Burton listened with rapt intensity, scribbling notes in her pristine pocketbook. Noakes and Doyle, meanwhile, rolled their eyes when they thought Markham wasn't looking.

There was a gentle tap at the door and a tall woman came into the room. Thick braids of wheat-coloured hair were coiled round her head in an old-fashioned style which somehow suited her statuesque beauty. Her eyes were blue and clear as crystal, her figure – in a simple wrap dress – superb. Self-consciously, Noakes and Doyle began clearing their throats and fiddling with their ties while Burton surveyed the intruder with territorial defensiveness.

'I'm Anna Sladen,' the newcomer said. It was a beautiful voice, thought Markham. Flute-like and melodious.

She held up a hand deprecatingly. 'I can see you're all done in, but I just wanted to introduce myself. I'm the clinical psychologist in charge of the Research Centre. That's the suite of rooms at the far end of the corridor,' she added by way of explanation. There was genuine sadness in her voice as she said, 'What happened to Jon was awful.' She hesitated. 'He lived for his work ... a pioneer in many ways.'

Discussion of Doctor Warr's legacy could wait, Markham decided. But in the meantime, it was good to feel at least one member of the medical staff was an ally.

'Thank you, Ms Sladen,' he said, the handsome features alight with real warmth. 'We'll be conducting interviews tomorrow and looking at the intensive care unit.'

Was it his imagination, or had the psychologist stiffened?

Her voice suddenly expressionless, Anna Sladen bade them goodnight and slipped away.

'Well,' Noakes smacked his lips appreciatively. 'I bet none of the crazies minds getting up close and personal with *her.*'

For once, nobody corrected him.

'C'mon, Benny Hill,' Doyle chaffed him affectionately. 'Let's get off.'

Burton's nose was already buried in a tome of doorstop dimensions. *Psychopathy in the Modern Era.*

Good luck with that, luv, thought Noakes sourly.

Aloud, he said, 'We c'n drop you off, boss.'

'Will you be all right, Kate?' asked Markham, ever the gentleman. 'Don't make a night of it, will you.'

'I'm fine, sir. This place never sleeps.'

Outside in the forecourt, looking back at the hospital, bathed in a pallid nimbus from strategically placed floodlights, those words came back to him like a warning.

This place never sleeps.

Distrustfully, he wondered if he could breach its defences.

4

Phantom Threads

WHEN TUESDAY MORNING DAWNED, it felt like coming to the surface of the water after deep sea diving.

It had been a restless night. Eventually, so as not to disturb Olivia with his tossing and turning, Markham crept into his study and watched dawn come up over the neighbouring municipal cemetery, ranks of headstones and memorials emerging palely into view from the morning mist.

It was a quirk of Markham's to welcome this proximity to the dead. The third floor apartment's view of the cemetery was the main reason he had moved to The Sweepstakes, a complex of upmarket apartments and townhouses at the end of Bromgrove Park, off Bromgrove Avenue. The ghosts of murdered men, women and children sometimes seemed more vivid than the world around him, for they were all still alive to him.

Were there any graves at the Newman, he wondered. The old asylums like Broadmoor had their cemeteries, because that was the last stop for some poor souls who rotted away there and had a pauper's burial. Modern special hospitals – those high-tech hangars with their air locks and airport-like scanners – presumably did things differently.

But what about the hopeless cases? Were they destined to remain in the Newman till the recording angel said 'time no longer'? Was some hidden corner of that NASA-style compound reserved for unsanctified outcasts like Mikey Belcher? Or would they only finally find freedom when their ashes were scattered to the four winds, like Hindley or Brady?

He shivered. Olivia would say he was being thoroughly morbid. But David Belcher's face had haunted his dreams. In his sleep, he followed Belcher along unnaturally bright corridors to a glass sliding door. On the other side of the door was an operating theatre where a white-clad patient lay strapped to a gurney, surrounded by gowned and masked figures like hieratic friezes on some ancient monolith. '*Look there,*' Belcher urged. '*Don't you see?*' As he spoke these words, one of the figures detached itself from the tableau and began to walk towards them. The figure lowered his surgical mask and Markham recognized the features of Chief Superintendent Philip Rees. He was saying something behind the glass – his lips were moving – but Markham couldn't hear what it was. Then a chasm suddenly opened beneath his feet and he was falling.... After that, there was nothing more. Belcher, the operating room and the patient on the bed were gone.

Markham thought back to his meeting with the Chief Super on Sunday, shortly after Jonathan Warr's body was discovered.

Rees was crisply imperturbable, the epitome of executive efficiency, his square-jawed good looks set off by pristine pips and epaulettes. No different from usual. 'Doctor Warr was an eminent practitioner in his field and a valued member of the police authority consultative panel.' His encomium – as brief as it was sensible – showed no self-consciousness.

There was nothing tangible to go on. Nothing apart from those lethal little slips of the tongue in minutes from the Newman's patients' council.

There's a copper knows ... the top man ... owns the place ... Magnum....

Magnum.

Rees's station nickname. An ironic nod to his uber-manliness.

And there it was in the mouth of a patient.

Deranged rodomontade? Or something more sinister?

Muriel Noakes, with her infallible nose for the false note, for the single detail a hair's breadth off centre, had felt it too.

Too much at home, she had sniffed about Rees's demeanour at the hospital's Open Day.

Was it 'access all areas' for Rees and, if so, why? How had he insinuated himself into the Newman? If he roamed the corridors, who gave him the keys?

Markham reminded himself he would have to be careful. Who would believe dangerous mentally ill patients over a police officer of Rees's pedigree, holder of the Queen's Police Medal for distinguished service?

No-one.

If Rees *was* involved in abuse, then hospital staff were most likely complicit and would now close ranks.

Birds of a feather.

Was Doctor Jonathan Warr part of the conspiracy? And why did he have to die?

No answers came to Markham as he sat in the raw morning light turning things over and over in his mind.

Coffee, he decided. Strong and black. The sovereign remedy for insomnia and jaded senses. And then off to the *Gazette* to speak to Noakes's 'slippery customer'.

Once out of the apartment, with the cold clear air blowing freshly over his face, Markham felt the violence of his agitation begin to subside.

Present fears are less than horrible imaginings.

His eyes wandered one last time from The Sweepstakes to the sprawling cemetery by its side – rested there thoughtfully, as he watched the feeble wintery sun warming the sleepers in that quiet earth.

His superstitious fears clung to him out of doors, as they had clung to him in his study in the chill early hours. Impatiently, he strode briskly towards the garages at the rear of the apartment block as though by that means he could outrun them.

Pete Darlington's cubicle in the *Gazette*'s offices was almost as frowsy as Noakes's workstation. With his mop top hair and anaemic weediness, the young reporter possessed a certain waifish vulnerability which no doubt stood him in good stead when it came to winkling out confidences from vulnerable members of the public. Puffing away on an e-cig, he eyed them warily.

'Look, gents, even if I knew anything about this so-called tip-off, I wouldn't be able to tell you.' He assumed an expression of candid ingenuousness. 'Gotta protect my sources, y'see.'

George Noakes was not a man to be propitiated by 'the soft answer which turneth away wrath'.

'Bollocks to your sources,' he grunted. 'You c'n come off your high horse an' all.' He fixed the shrinking youth with a piggy stare. 'You used to diddle my Nat behind the bike sheds. I know all about *you*.'

Markham reflected that this was likely true of more than a few acned youths in Bromgrove.

Still, the shaft appeared to have hit its mark. The scrawny journalist dropped his eyes.

'Okay, so what if I did make a phone call to your lot?' he said finally, before adding with a touch of defiance, 'It's not illegal.'

'No, Mr Darlington, it's not,' Markham said quietly. 'But with a consultant psychiatrist from the Newman Hospital turning up murdered, we are now taking a keen interest in this tale of disappearing patients.'

Darlington sat down with a defeated air. Markham nodded to Noakes, who promptly appropriated two chairs from adjoining cubicles.

'There's prob'ly nothing in it. I was dating this dippy bird from the hospital. Receptionist ... secretary ... summat like that.'

'Ah.' Light began to dawn. *Hayley*, thought Markham and saw the same conviction reflected in Noakes's eyes.

'We'd been watching *The Shining* an' were just swapping daft stories – trying to scare each other shitless. We'd had a bit to drink ...'

'Go on,' said Noakes, not unkindly.

'Well, she said summat about spooky stuff happening where she worked. I asked what kind of spooky and she said there were patients went into the hospital who never came out ... as in no-one ever saw them again ... Look, we were a bit out of it ... she dared me to ring the cop shop, so I did.'

Darlington squirmed uncomfortably.

'It was just a bit of a laugh, that's all.'

He took another long drag of the e-cig. Uppity little git. Noakes's expression was as eloquent as if he had said the words aloud.

'There's always been stories about the Newman.' The reporter looked hopefully at Markham. 'I thought it was a load of baloney, but ... well, you never know ... I made the phone call but that was the end of it, so I figured there was nuffink doing. Me and the bird broke up soon after.'

'Did your girlfriend say where this story came from?' Markham raked Darlington with a keen glance.

'Look, it was a load of moonshine. She just wanted to get a reaction. Showing off, like. That was the thing with Hayley, she liked having secrets and playing games. Made her feel she was more than just a dogsbody, but it was all a big tease.' He looked at the telephone on his desk as though willing it to ring. 'I got the feeling she may've had a snoop at some paperwork ... confidential stuff she didn't ought to see.'

Minutes from the patients' council. Or paperwork from the abuse investigation.

'Was there gossip amongst the hospital staff?'

'Dunno,' was the sulky reply.

'Look, sunshine,' Noakes got up and loomed over the reporter menacingly in his best impersonation of the Sweeney. 'We've got one dead doc. No face an' not a lot left down below after the foxes were finished with him.'

Darlington looked as though he might throw up.

'For Chrissake,' he said with a note of desperation in his reedy treble. 'It's a long time ago.' Noakes showed no sign of budging. 'I got the impression it was more like a joke,' the reporter stammered.

'A joke,' Markham repeated stonily.

'Well,' beads of sweat were forming along Darlington's upper lip. 'Staff banter.' Clutching at straws, he blurted, 'Y'know ... like Fred an' Rose West when they told their kids "If you don't behave, you'll end up under the patio" ... kinda, "look out, the bogeyman's coming to get you" ...'

'Is this for real?' Noakes sounded bemused.

'Straight up. There was some old biddy – one of the volun-teers, Linda something – told them to put a sock in it cos of it being garbage and disrespectful to the patients. But the rest of 'em had a laugh now and again.' He looked from Noakes to Markham and back again. 'There was no real harm in it,' he concluded lamely.

Gallows humour, thought Markham. You'd hear much the same in the CID canteen any night of the week.

The DI contemplated Darlington with distaste.

'Don't leave Bromgrove any time soon.'

He didn't raise his voice but there was no mistaking the biting undertone.

'What a prince.'

Noakes relieved his feelings by kicking Markham's tyres.

'Jus' checking the pressure ... there were a few pot holes back there.'

The DI discreetly waited till they were on their way for Noakes to unburden himself.

'Spotty little nerk. When I think of him makin' free with our Nat.'

Again, Markham reflected that Natalie Noakes was no doubt prodigal of her favours, given the regularity with which she was spied propping up the bar in Bromgrove's less salu-brious nightclubs. Not that her blindly-doting father saw his offspring as anything other than perfect. 'Can't help being popular, can she?' he bristled at an ill-advised quip from DC Doyle. Since then his colleagues had learned to tread carefully round the subject.

Markham shot Noakes an affectionate sideways glance. The DS appeared positively dapper compared with Pete Darlington, but the combination of beige cords, blue plaid shirt, maroon jacket and bilious mauve tie made it look as though he had dressed in the dark. Currently losing the battle of the bulge – even though he and Muriel were keen ballroom dancers with several trophies to their credit – he struggled to fasten the passenger seatbelt across his portly girth.

Markham waited for the inevitable plea which was not long in coming.

'How about a bacon sarnie to put us on till elevenses?' the DS suggested, spotting Greggs on their right as they approached the town centre cul de sac where Bromgrove Council had its offices.

'Wouldn't hurt you to skip breakfast, Noakesy,' the DI commented mildly but drew up nonetheless.

Watching the DS amble happily towards his fast food mecca, Markham thought back over the interview with Darlington.

Unproductive as it was, there was the uneasy feeling of being behind the beat – of having missed something.

Markham's eyes felt gritty with fatigue, his mind drifting back to last night's dream, wandering deeper and deeper into the heart of the Newman ... until, suddenly, there was Noakes at the car window jiggling a brown paper bag in his face.

'C'mon, Guv. Grub's up.'

In fact, the coffee and greasy comfort food gave him a much-needed fillip, while Noakes was in seventh heaven.

'Their bacon rolls are deffo the best,' he announced finally.

'Sausage, bacon and egg in your case.' Markham smiled indulgently at his subordinate's sheepish expression. Then his face grew serious again. 'Right, stir your stumps, Sergeant. We'll roust Ted Cartwright from wherever he's lurking, then I want to get back to the Newman.'

The DS looked at him closely. 'What's biting you, Guv?'

'I can't put my finger on it,' the DI replied slowly. 'Just a feeling that something's wrong ...'

Noakes had a healthy respect for his boss's hunches, so made no further demur and the two men headed towards the ugly cinder block complex in search of the council's legal services department.

If stonewalling was an Olympic event, then Ted Cartwright would win a gold medal, thought Noakes sourly, as he watched the slimy solicitor parry every one of Markham's questions with a convenient memory lapse. 'I can't quite recall ...' 'I don't seem to recollect ...' 'That escapes me just for the moment ...' A geyser of evasions.

Immoveable force meets immoveable object.

There was something stoat-like about the squat solicitor with his well-cut suit and grey buzz cut gleaming with some rich dressing. Like a well-fed mafioso.

'Now that the Health Trust and other professional bodies are investigating the Newman's management practices, any issue of—' here Cartwright injected a note of incredulity, '—missing patients is obviously *sub judice*. That means—'

'I'm aware of what *sub judice* means, Mr Cartwright.' Markham's voice was deadly as he cut through the legal flannel. 'This is a murder investigation, and any pertinent information that you possess will therefore be *shared*.'

'I'll need to consult the files to refresh my recollection, Inspector.' Cartwright's tongue darted out, lizard-like, to lick thick fleshy lips. 'Perhaps a memo ...'

When in doubt, procrastinate.

'If it's not too much trouble.'

As he registered the sarcasm, the solicitor's eyes narrowed to slits.

Don Corleone, thought Noakes. The guvnor'll end up sleeping with the fishes at this rate.

'Chief Superintendent Philip Rees is Gold Commander on the case, Mr Cartwright, and I can fax you a list of personnel.'

What response would Philip Rees's name elicit?

Something skittered at the back of those ferrety eyes and was gone.

But Markham knew he hadn't imagined it.

The look of recognition and something else.

Fear?

'He's a gangster, that one,' was Noakes's verdict as they exited the building.

Gangster, gigolo and all round good-for-nothing, Markham concurred silently.

'D'you see his mug when you mentioned the Chief Super? Crapping his pants.'

Noakes was plundering the furthest reaches of the vernacular today.

'Indeed, Sergeant. That got a reaction all right.' He paused by the car. 'If Rees is putting the squeeze on Cartwright, then why and how?' In his mind's eye he saw again the shifty expression on those saurian features. 'One thing's for sure. There's a connection between those two that goes deeper than local authority business.'

The hard brightness of the winter sky seemed to mock his indecision. 'Right, Noakes,' he said, 'back to the Newman.'

After their excursion outdoors, the hospital felt like a giant greenhouse with its airless, smothering atmosphere. Noakes wrenched at his tie as though it was strangling him.

But on the surface, all was tranquil. Like a torpid mill pond.

A different receptionist was on duty; mousy, deferential and apparently awed to the point of muteness. Markham wondered if she had been warned not to talk to them.

In no time at all, they were through the checks and identification processes.

'Can you direct us to the intensive care ward, please?' Markham said firmly, registering with interest the flash of panic in her eyes.

'I'll just ring through to Ms Holder, Inspector,' she said faintly.

'By all means,' he responded equably.

Clickety-clack, clickety-clack. The sound of Claire Holder's high heels.

The managing director – clad in a cobalt blue power suit – arrived so quickly, the DI figured there must have been an All Ports Alert out for himself and Noakes.

She seemed nervous, he thought, keeping up a non-stop stream of inconsequential chit-chat as she conducted them along the corridor that he remembered from before ... with one subtle difference. The framed photograph that had arrested his attention on their last visit was gone as though it had never hung there. As though the enigmatic landscape with its lonely pavilions and eerie signature had melted into the ether. In its place hung a bold brash piece of modern art – squares and rectangles in clashing primary colours. A Mondrian reproduction by the look of it. Markham decided he didn't much care for it.

Once through the swing doors, they found themselves blanketed by an even deeper hush, as though in a decompression chamber. The passage was lined on both sides with stout locked doors bisected by louvred panels. A heavily fortified nursing station occupied the far end.

A panopticon with no visible signs of life.

But Markham sensed deranged faces, pressed against the glass panels, leering at himself and Noakes. His skin prickled as though the patients' stares were so many poisoned darts.

Once at the nursing station, they were greeted by a dark young man of Mediterranean appearance whom Claire Holder introduced as Doctor Lopez. She didn't bother with the two brawny orderlies who watched impassively with incurious eyes. A middle-aged woman with short blonde hair was similarly beneath her notice.

Ushering them through hermetically sealed glass doors behind the station, Doctor Lopez showed them the comfortably furnished recreation area where a couple of men promenaded ponderously like lethargic giants, ignoring a television that was blaring in the corner. Behind the recreation lounge, Doctor Lopez told them, were the female section and two therapy rooms.

Markham felt his heart rate slow.

No sign of the mysterious operating theatre of his dream.

No gurney.

No gowned figures.

They walked back to the nursing station, Doctor Lopez discoursing amicably on the tilt from custodial to rehabilitative principles in acute cases. Meanwhile, the managing director's impatient foot-tapping and general demeanour indicated her pressing desire to bring the visit to a close.

Finally, the young doctor came to a halt. 'Feel free to ask me anything you like, gentlemen.'

'Actually, Doctor Lopez, I wonder if it would be possible for me to see a patient. Mikey Belcher.'

An invisible signal passed between the doctor and managing director.

'I'm afraid that won't be possible just at the moment, Inspector. Mikey's had a difficult morning.'

'Oh?'

'He's in seclusion now for his own safety.'

'Why, what's he gone and done?'

Up till now, Noakes's curranty eyes had been like swivelling lenses, paying sharp attention to everything round him. But now they narrowed uncompromisingly on Doctor Lopez's face as he posed this inconvenient question.

'Seclusion is only used as a matter of clinical necessity, Sergeant, not as a punishment. It isn't a question of Mikey having "done" anything, but rather a way for us to find the best way of helping him.' Doctor Lopez's manner was emollient, but he had one eye on the managing director whose folded arms suggested access to Belcher was no-go.

As they stood in their awkward huddle, there was a minor commotion behind them. The mousy receptionist stood there twisting her hands.

'What is it, Moira?' Claire Holder snapped. 'For God's sake, don't just stand there looking like a stranded guppy fish. *Say something.*'

'It's Hayley,' she stuttered.

Something clicked in the DI's brain.

Those words of the erstwhile paramour.

'She liked having secrets and playing games. Made her feel she was more than just a dogsbody, but it was all a big tease.'

Markham felt the cold clutch of anxiety at his heart.

'What about Hayley?' he said urgently.

'Well, she missed her shift this morning an' no-one's been able to get hold of her.... Her mobile's off.' The receptionist gulped for breath. 'Human Resources checked with her flat-mate ... she says Hayley didn't come home last night.' More hand-wringing. 'It's not like her.'

Markham and Noakes exchanged a long look, each thinking of the pint-sized charmer and her artless prattle.

Markham turned to Claire Holder.

'I want everywhere on lockdown as of now. And I need a floorplan of the facility.' His tone made it clear he expected immediate compliance.

He turned to the DS. 'Round up Burton and Doyle. Then find out who was the last person to see Hayley yesterday. She was friends with one of the volunteers ... Linda something ... see if she knows anything.'

The group scattered.

Behind locked doors, in one of those deranged brains, there were memories that needed to be subdued, to be tranquilized by calm and eventually blotted out altogether.

As if nothing had happened.

5

The Sleep of Reason

MARKHAM'S TEAM ASSEMBLED IN the incident room. Courteously but firmly, Kate Burton took the floorplan that Claire Holder had brought before steering her towards the door.

'See if you can round up the volunteers and any of Hayley's colleagues who saw her last thing yesterday.'

Beneath the pan stick, the managing director's face had turned white, arrogance replaced by sheer terror.

'You don't think whoever killed Jon's got her, do you?' Her face twisted. 'Poor little thing … she hadn't begun to live.'

Burton suddenly liked the woman much better for that remark. Gently she said, 'We're not jumping to any conclusions, Ms Holder, and nor should you.'

After the director had left on her errand, Burton rejoined her colleagues and rolled out the floorplan. Intently, they hunched over it.

Rooms were represented by rows of small squares, with numbers neatly printed inside them.

'There's a key at the bottom,' Markham murmured, scanning the list of names. 'Hold on a minute.' The DI's forefinger paused.

'What is it, sir?' Burton tried to see what had arrested the boss's attention.

'It says *Morgue* on here....'

Despite the stuffiness of the room, at those words an icicle trickled inch by inch down Burton's back, as if cold fingers were touching her – cold, softly creeping fingers.

'*Morgue?*' Noakes was equally discomfited. 'But it's a mental ... er, special ... hospital...' His voice trailed off uncertainly.

'Presumably they have to be prepared in case there's a sudden death,' Markham said slowly. 'They'd need a side room or somewhere private.'

'To keep out the gawkers,' DC Doyle concurred solemnly. 'I mean, one of the patients might freak out if they saw a dead body getting hauled off.'

'Bromgrove General's just next door,' Burton said. 'So, if someone dies here, staff can get the body moved quickly without anyone getting upset.'

Noakes was thoughtful.

'Wonder how many of 'em in here topped themselves.'

His question hung in the air, and the heavy stillness was more oppressive than ever.

They were interrupted by Claire Holder and another woman whose kind, plump face was creased with anxiety.

'Ah, it's Mrs Harelock, isn't it ... one of the befrienders?' Markham remembered the newcomer from the previous day's trip to the hospital café. Middle-aged, with faded, pretty features and silver hair becomingly styled and waved, she had all the warmth that the managing director so conspicuously lacked.

'That's right, Inspector. I met you and the sergeant yesterday.'

'Hayley said you're the Newman's longest serving volunteer.'

Linda Harelock looked pleased.

'Well, after my husband died, I had a lot of time on my hands and wanted to give something back.' Clearly, this wasn't a woman who enjoyed the spotlight. In a quiet, self-effacing manner, she continued. 'You want to know about Hayley, Inspector. She came into the café for a cup of tea at around 4.30 after her shift had finished.'

'Was there anything out of the ordinary that you noticed?'

'Nothing. We had a quick chat. She was planning a night in.' A fond expression crossed her face. 'With one of her box sets ... some Scandinavian thriller or other.'

'Was anyone else in the café?'

'I think Moira – that's one of the other receptionists – was in there as well ...'

Markham turned to Claire Holder. 'Can you get hold of Moira for us quickly, please?'

He smiled at Linda Harelock, but the smile couldn't disguise the strain in his eyes.

'What about boyfriends, Mrs Harelock? Was Hayley seeing someone?'

'She told me she was "off men", Inspector,' Linda Harelock said. There was a rueful note in the woman's voice. 'I think her love life was what you'd call a car crash. There was some lad from the *Gazette*, but it didn't work out. Before that, she was dating a paralegal at the Council.' The volunteer sighed. 'Hayley came from a broken home, so I think she was desperate for security.'

'Was she involved with anyone here?' Burton asked.

'At the Newman?' The woman was startled. 'Not as far as I know.'

'What about Doctor Warr, luv?'

Trust Noakes to detonate the H bomb.

Linda Harelock looked confused.

'Doctor Warr? D'you mean a ... *romantic* involvement?'

'Well, glamorous older guy ... a doctor ... mebbe the white coat turned her on ...'

Observing the pinched look on Burton's face, Noakes added defiantly, 'Happens all the time. Didn't Princess Di say she had a thing for doctors...?'

This elicited a good-natured laugh from the volunteer.

'Hayley would have regarded Doctor Warr as positively *ancient*, Sergeant. And in any event—' She stopped short, as though fearful of saying too much. Markham was sure Claire Holder's name had been on her lips, but she had remembered herself just in time.

The woman raised a nervous hand to her hair, smoothing out a non-existent tangle.

'As I say, Hayley had given up on men. Her only sweetheart here was Ernie.'

'Ernie?' Markham's expression cleared. 'Oh yes, your head porter.'

Linda Harelock's face fell. 'God, he'll be devastated if anything happens to her.' Looking anxiously towards the door, she added, 'I should go to him really – before he hears it from someone else. They're great friends ... she looks after his dog ... pops round for a chat.... She's got no real family to speak of, so Ernie's like a father figure.'

Grandfather more like, thought Noakes, but kept his mouth shut.

'Of course, Mrs Harelock, and thank you for your help.'

'I'm not sure I *was* much help, Inspector.'

As the volunteer was leaving, she almost collided with Claire Holder and the mousy receptionist they had encountered earlier.

'Here she is.,' The managing director shot a minatory glare at the cowed-looking girl trailing behind her.

The girl's appearance was even more downtrodden and dispirited than Markham remembered. She appeared fearful and kept peering at the corners of the room as though she half expected to see something creeping along the wall towards her. Definitely the nervy type.

'There's nothing to be frightened of, Moira.' Markham spoke in his friendliest manner. 'You're not in any trouble.' At this, the receptionist's eyes wandered to Claire Holder, but she stopped biting her fingernails and gave the DI a watery smile.

'Mrs Harelock was able to tell us Hayley was in the café yesterday around 4.30 at the end of her shift. She thinks you were there too. If that's right, then you might be able to give us an idea how Hayley looked … if she was her usual self, or if there was something on her mind.'

The girl blinked, looking round apprehensively at the four officers.

'Likes a cuppa and a chinwag at the end of the day does she, luv?' Noakes's tone was conspiratorial. 'Me too, though it's not the same without a ciggie.'

The down-to-earth comment, and the wink that accompanied it, did the trick.

'Oh, Hayley gave up a while ago. Her ex got her on to them e-cigs.'

Noakes turned even more confiding. 'Oh aye. Cost a packet, they do, with all that fiddly gear. Bit girly, if you know what I mean.'

Burton made a restless movement, but Markham quelled her with a glance. Moira had lost her look of a rabbit caught in the headlights. That was Noakes's gift. As though by some mysterious alchemy, there was something in his blessedly normal

DNA which made the demons scuttle off into the woodwork.

'How did Hayley take the split with her ex?' Noakes contin-ued, with his air of unthreatening friendly interest, as if he and Moira were chatting in a queue at the bus stop.

'She was well rid, if you ask me. Real poser.' The succinct verdict was delivered with some venom.

'So, Hayley seemed okay when you saw her in the caff?' Noakes drew closer to the last sighting of the missing recep-tionist. Treating Moira to his bluffest grin, he added, 'Women pick up on signals – stuff that blokes don't notice. That's what my missus allus says.'

This appeal to her superior powers of observation embold-ened Moira.

'Well, she looked dead pleased with herself ...'

'Pleased with herself?'

'Like she'd found something out ...' Moira pulled up short, looking embarrassed by her own candour, but Noakes just nodded encouragingly. 'Like she knew something the rest of us didn't an' was one up.'

'So, she didn't give you any clues then?' The DS was very casual. 'D'you think it was personal ... new fella on the scene? Or summat to do with work? Was she in line for a promotion?' He grinned. 'Pay rise?'

'I don't think it was a promotion or anything like that,' Moira ventured tentatively.

Claire Holder's unnecessarily vigorous head shake made her views on the matter all too plain.

There was a pause.

'Did you see where Hayley went?' Noakes asked. 'D'you think she went straight home to slob in front of the telly? Or could she have been waiting for someone?'

Moira seemed to be thinking hard.

'Now I think of it, she glanced at her watch a couple of times,' the receptionist said finally. 'Almost as if she was watching out for someone. Like she had an appointment an' didn't want to be late.'

'But you didn't see anyone else around?'

'No. It was just me an' her in there. Linda clocked off after she served us. Hayley just said hiya to me and drank her tea. She didn't look like she was in the mood for a chat, so we sat for a bit. Then she waved and said see ya.' Moira's face crumpled. 'That was it. I didn't even look up when she went.' Producing a none too clean wad of tissue, she proceeded to blow her nose loudly.

'That was champion, luv.' Noakes clapped her on the shoulder. 'I know some of our lot,' he bestowed a significant look on DC Doyle, 'who couldn't have told us half what you jus' did. We could do with you in CID.' The feeble witticism earned him a tremulous smile. At a nod from Markham, Claire Holder escorted the tearful receptionist from the room.

'So, Hayley likely never left the hospital.' Noakes was now all business.

'Right.' Markham's face was sombre. 'I think she knew something about Doctor Warr's death ... was planning to meet someone.'

'Blackmail,' Burton said flatly.

'Looks very much like it.' The DI's eyes were speculative. 'Pete Darlington, the ex, said she liked secrets and playing games.'

'Proper out of her depth, then,' DC Doyle said.

'Yes, she wouldn't have realized the danger till it was too late.'

Burton followed Markham's gaze back to the plan. The chill struck her again.

Claire Holder reappeared.

'I want to see the room marked *Morgue,*' Markham said without preamble.

The managing director's reaction took them all by surprise. A ripple passed across her features; her complexion flushed all over, then turned ashy pale once again. Drawing out a linen handkerchief, she passed it rapidly over her face where perspiration had gathered thickly at the hairline.

'Does that room hold some special significance for you?' the DI asked quietly. 'Were you perhaps in the habit of meeting someone there?'

'Jon and I sometimes snatched a moment when we wanted to be private.' She met his eyes almost defiantly.

And you got a kick out of it, you sick bitch, thought Noakes.

'I'm not aware of it having ever been used for mortuary purposes in my time here.' She seemed to force the words past an obstacle in her throat. 'But it had a bit of a reputation. There were ghost stories and the like.' A rictus grin accompanied this admission.

'So, staff would've avoided the room?' Burton's eyes narrowed on the director's face.

'As far as I know, yes,' came the stiff response.

'Take me to it,' was all Markham said.

In lockdown, the hospital struck Markham as having a sepulchral quality which was grimly appropriate given the half-life led by patients behind its walls. Again, there was that oxygen-less sensation which left him feeling light-headed.

They passed by doors, staircases and passages, a sense of foreboding floating around and over them so that it seemed part of the atmosphere. As the course of Markham's thoughts drew him more and more completely from outward things, he wondered if the inmates of the forensic unit ever came out of those cells like the dead from their graves. And, once free of their fetters, what might they not do?

'Here it is.' Claire Holder's voice broke upon his thoughts.

Nothing to see here, move along.

It was a white-painted, windowless room with a hospital trolley bed in the centre, a white sheet draped neatly across it. Medical cabinets lined the walls and a sluice unit occupied the left-hand corner.

Sterile, boring, unexceptional.

Markham was turning away when he heard 'Wassat?'

Noakes pointed to a stainless-steel hatch to the right of the door by which they had entered.

'Oh, that's just a service lift.' The managing director was dismissive. 'You know, like a dumb waiter. Must've been used to send supplies up from the basement at some time. It's under-ground garages down there now, but there were storerooms on the old site.'

The big untidy DS moved lightly as though afraid to wake a sleeper.

'It's not too small, boss. She's jus' a scrap of a thing ...'

No bigger than a child.

'Get it open, Noakes.'

As though looking down from above in an out-of-body experience, Markham watched his DS prise the sliding doors apart.

Hayley was inside, wedged upright in the foetal position, knees tucked beneath her chin. Her right profile, turned towards them, was serene as a madonna's, the eyes closed.

The only signs of trauma were two livid bruises either side of her neck, visible through the strands of long blonde hair.

'*Sweet Jesus,*' breathed Claire Holder in horror.

Burton and Doyle stared as if transfixed.

Noakes's eyes were full of tears as he looked at the body. 'Poor little girl,' he said gruffly, contemplating their erstwhile chatterbox guide, 'poor stupid little girl.' And then, as if to himself, 'Why didn't you come to us, luv? Why didn't you tell us?' Angrily, he wiped his sleeve across his eyes. Then he took a juddering breath.

Meanwhile, mobile in hand, Markham set the wheels of a second murder investigation in motion.

Some time later, after the police pathologist had authorized removal of the body, Markham's team reconvened in the late Doctor Warr's office. Considerably less luxurious in its appointments than Claire Holder's, it betrayed nothing of the man's personality, being devoid of any personal touches save for a cactus sitting forlornly on the untidy desk. Every surface overflowed with manuals and journals, and an extensive medical library was displayed on floor to ceiling bookshelves. There was no window, but a domed skylight relieved the laboratory feel of the room.

In response to the DI's interrogative glance, Burton was quick to assure him. 'Nothing doing in here, sir. We went through the desk and filing cabinets. Nada.'

Markham walked slowly along the bookshelves, murmuring aloud.

Techniques for Brain Disorders. The History of Transorbital Leucotomy. Psychosurgery and The Limits of Medicine. Cutting of the Mind. Desperate Cures: The Lobotomy in Context.

'Perhaps I can help shed some light, Inspector.'

Anna Sladen stood at the door, her queenly good looks more pronounced than ever against the dreary backdrop of Doctor Warr's office. It was the kind of beauty which seemed to be thrown into relief by simplicity, a plain blue dress, swathed about her waist, enhancing its fluid curves. The golden hair, looped into a snood at the back of her head, gave her the look of an Arthurian heroine from one of Markham's childhood treasuries.

Where'd *she* pop up from? Burton was poised to intercept the intruder, but Markham held up a restraining hand.

'It's all right, Sergeant. Come in, Ms Sladen.'

'I heard about Hayley,' she said, the musical voice falling like balm on his ears. 'And I know you'll get whoever did that to her.'

Strange, thought the DI, how those few words of trust should mean so much to him.

'Thank you.'

'You were wondering about Jon's library,' she said.

'Yes. Doctor Warr seemed to have somewhat specialized interests.'

'He was a keen historian. Read everything he could get his hands on about surgical techniques for the mentally ill.'

'Like lobotomies.'

'You know something about such procedures, Inspector?'

'I know they were in vogue in the forties and fifties. Drilling into the brain, wasn't it?'

'In essence, yes. Psychosurgery was pretty much the last chance saloon for the most acute cases – schizophrenics and manic depressives. Some of it was quite primitive, like the "ice pick operation" where they went in through the bone above the eye.'

Transorbital.

Warr had been stabbed through the eye. Mutilation post mortem.

Could there be a connection?

Noakes was interested.

'Did it work then, this poking around in folks' heads? Did it cure 'em?'

'That was the tragedy.' She grimaced. 'It was highly experimental and results were very mixed. Sure, some patients were more docile and less prone to outbursts, but as people they were pretty much gone ... zombies, if you like.'

'But hospitals aren't still doing that kind of operation, are they? I mean, not with all the drugs they've got now.' As usual, Burton wanted to be clear about everything.

Anna Sladen looked uncomfortable.

'Well, there were still variations on the lobotomy being carried out in the seventies and eighties,' she said warily. 'And psychosurgery is still used for conditions like OCD.'

'Think I'd rather jus' be a hoarder,' said Noakes. 'Better'n some medico taking chunks out of me.'

'It'd be open to abuse, wouldn't it, that kind of procedure?' Burton's face was troubled.

'True.' Again, the look of unease. 'Say you had a relative who looked likely to embarrass the family, then a lobotomy was one way of removing the problem. Erasing the record.' She paused. 'But afterwards, because the doctors kept cutting away, destroying larger and larger areas of brain, what was left would be hardly recognizable.' Her sensitive face was sorrowful. 'Like a painting that had been brutally slashed.'

Doyle looked as though he was going to be sick.

'Of course, now there are strict rules governing consent,' the psychologist said hastily, 'but it wasn't always the case, and there were some terrible stories along the way.'

Markham looked thoughtfully at the bookshelves.

Erasing the record. Terrible stories. Abuses.

Like a depth charge in his subconscious, the DI felt sure he had just learned something important....

'Thank you,' he said simply. 'You've brought Doctor Warr out of the shadows. He feels less of an enigma now.'

Flushing a little, Anna Sladen turned away. A shy smile and she was gone.

'She's all right for a trick cyclist,' Noakes said after the door had shut behind her. 'All that stuff about brains being turned to jelly ... d'you think that's why Doctor Warr got chopped about, Guv?'

'Well, you know how I feel about coincidences, Sergeant,' came the grim reply.

'Bit suspicious, though,' Burton put in, 'how she wanted to tell us Warr was a hack and slash merchant.'

'Good point, Kate. We need to take a closer look at Doctor Warr's research interests.'

She coloured up.

Daft bint. She's still got it bad, thought Noakes beadily. Now she'd be boring them all rigid quoting from that pervs' manual or whatever the hell it was....

'Right.' The DI's voice interrupted his musings. 'You're with me, Noakes. DCI Sidney needs to be briefed.'

There was a very audible whimper.

'I know, I know.' Markham sighed. 'The DCI'll want to pin this on the nearest available psychopath PDQ.' Wearily, he continued, 'I think it's a whole heap more complicated, not to say murkier, than that.'

'I'll correlate patient and staff movements for the last twenty-four hours, sir.' Burton was champing at the bit. 'On a spreadsheet tracker,' she said in a tone that suggested life could hold no greater bliss.

Jesus wept. Noakes studiously avoided meeting Doyle's eye.

'Excellent. Doyle, you can finish taking the staff statements.'

*

Both men were glad to get out of the hospital.

Markham imagined lunatic eyes upon them as they walked away into the swiftly darkening afternoon, rage flashing somewhere in the depths of the building like lightning across a troubled sky. The conviction was so strong, that halfway across the courtyard he whirled around, expecting to see the face of evil pass like a blanched moon across one of those reinforced glass windows.

But nothing stirred, and the Newman kept its secrets close.

6

A Cold Front

'"The condemned man ate a hearty meal."'

Markham grinned at the expression on Noakes's face as they sat across from each other in the station canteen, the DS boggling as his boss tucked into sausage and chips.

'I can't face the DCI on an empty stomach,' the DI admitted. 'Or maybe I'm just reacting to the Newman.' He shuddered. 'There's something so glazed ... so cellophane-wrapped about that place. It makes me want to kick over the traces.'

'You should do it more often, Guv,' Noakes grunted. 'They do a mean steak and kidney pie in here.'

'That would be living dangerously.' In every sense of the word, Markham thought to himself as he contemplated the grubby tables.

He pushed his plate away.

'How are we going to play it with the DCI, boss?'

Intimations of nausea circled round Markham's digestive system.

'We just sit and suck it up, Sergeant. Going on past form, I imagine he'll stick with the status quo.' Wearily, he elucidated.

'That means pinning the murders on our old friend the "bushy haired stranger" rather than daring to insinuate that anyone at the Health Trust could possibly be involved.'

'Cos Sidney plays golf with 'em,' Noakes observed bluntly.

'That's about the size of it.'

For a wistful moment, the two men silently pondered the Shangri-La of a world without DCI Sidney before Markham got to his feet. 'C'mon, Sergeant,' he sighed, 'best get it over with.'

Miss Peabody, Slimy Sid's irreproachably correct PA, fluttered round them, enlarged moth eyes scanning an appointments book which she clung on to for dear life.

'I don't know, Inspector ... that is, he may be able to fit you in ... perhaps I could ...'

Eying Noakes warily as though she suspected he might not be fully house-trained, the secretary sidled towards the door of Sidney's inner sanctum and disappeared.

'Always looks at me as if she thinks I'm going to pinch the silver or summat,' the DS grumbled.

Reading the runes from Miss Peabody's appearance was something of an art form, Markham reflected. On this occasion, he judged that the DCI's mood had taken a sharp turn downwards.

Once they were ushered into the Presence, it became rapidly apparent to the DI that this conclusion was correct. No offer of tea or coffee was forthcoming, and from the baleful glances directed at Noakes, it was clear the DCI was inventorying fresh causes for complaint. Irritably, he scratched at an outbreak of eczema which mottled his sallow cheeks above the salt and pepper goatee. Somehow, even with the buzz cut and designer beard, he managed to look more like a suburban accountant than the head of CID.

'... The way this is managed could have a major impact on public confidence in the police.'

Oops. It was always risky to tune out mid-spiel. Now the DCI was glaring at him with unmistakable hostility.

'Maintaining public confidence. Absolutely our priority, sir.'

Parroting back Sidney's own words usually worked as a stalling tactic.

'The prospect of dangerously unstable mental patients on the rampage ... well, I need hardly spell it out.'

God, here it was bang on cue. The bushy haired stranger. You had to say this for him, Sidney never disappointed.

'With respect, sir.' Sidney looked as though he suspected this was Markham's semaphore for the exact opposite. 'Scrutinizing former and current service users will obviously be our most urgent priority.' Obviously. 'But presumably we need to consider a possible connection with ... ongoing investigations ...'

The DCI's long-lived, wondering frown was something to behold.

'Ah, there's that *flair* of yours, Markham.' Sidney made it sound like a medical condition. 'A good thing of its kind, but mustn't let it ride you.' In a ghastly simulacrum of joviality, he forced a laugh. 'I'm confident we can trust the GMC and CQC to do their stuff.' Funny how the acronyms always tripped off the man's tongue, Markham thought savagely. 'No need for us to muddy the waters, Inspector.'

The DI gritted his teeth.

'There's also the missing persons investigation the DCC tasked me with, sir.'

Sidney patently didn't care to be reminded.

'Well, we all have our ... hobby horses,' he said with benign condescension, 'but I think you'll be heading up a blind alley,

Markham.' Clearly charmed by this metaphor, he repeated it. 'Nothing but a blind alley.'

With kamikaze desperation, Markham tried again.

'It just seems too much of a coincidence that there should be these concerns about the Newman,' Sidney shot him a gimlet-eyed look of pure loathing, 'at the same time as a consultant and receptionist turn up murdered.'

'Sexual psychosis.' With this gnomic pronouncement, the DCI sat back in his chair as if to say 'game, set and match'.

'What?'

'Attractive young female targeted by a predatory mental health patient.' Sidney shook his head sorrowfully. 'The public needs protecting from such individuals.'

'Why?' blurted Noakes. 'I mean, it's not like they're going anywhere.'

Sidney chose to ignore this interruption by the village idiot.

'What about Doctor Warr?' Markham was curious to see where this went.

'Ah, a case of transference, Markham.' Sidney switched to finger-wagging mode. 'The patient idealizes his psychiatrist as a father figure then kills him after a perceived rejection.'

'Doctor Warr's body was found outside the hospital, sir.'

'You should be looking at *ex*-patients in that case, or considering the possibility of a *shared delusion*.' With some complacency, he added, '*Folie* à *deux*, I think they call it.'

Well, thank you very much, Dr Freud.

'Talking of accomplices,' which Markham wasn't, 'you might want to check out that unsavoury character who's been operating some sort of vendetta against the hospital. Has a brother in the Newman, I believe.' Sidney nodded with profound sagacity. 'They say the apple never falls far from the tree.'

Do they?

Satisfied that he had bludgeoned the opposition into silence, Sidney continued. 'Or there's the fellow whose wife died after an … unfortunate … judgement call.'

Unfortunate. God in heaven.

'I think both Mr Belcher and Mr Hewitt can be ruled out for the second murder, sir, as this occurred within the hospital complex … it's unlikely either of them broke in and, in any event, one imagines their logical target would be medical personnel as opposed to a receptionist.'

'Ah, that's where the accomplice comes in. Someone on the inside.'

Markham could see that if the DCI was forced to relinquish his bushy haired stranger as prime suspect, then Belcher or Hewitt were next up.

'It's certainly one line of enquiry, sir,' he said non-committally.

Sidney looked at him suspiciously.

'You believe the murders are connected, Inspector?'

'As I say, sir, it feels too unlikely to be coincidence.'

'Distrust *feeling,* Markham. A trap for the unwary.'

God, if there was something worse than outright hostility, it was the faux paternalism.

'I believe that Doctor Warr was murdered because of his activities at the Newman, sir,' he said quietly, 'and that the receptionist Hayley had found out about it. He had some … unusual research interests.'

The stony silence which greeted this statement was hardly encouraging, but the DI persisted. 'It's possible there's a link to the malpractice inquiry and mispers, sir.'

The silence lengthened, threatening to become awkward, but Markham made no attempt to fill it. Crossing one elegant leg across the other, he feigned intense interest in the innumerable framed pictures of Sidney rubbing shoulders with a host of celebrities and civic worthies. No wonder station wags had christened his office the Hall of Fame.

Hold on a minute. Wasn't that a new addition to the collection?

Yes, there was the DCI hobnobbing with filthy rich Sir Jocelyn Hart, CEO of Bromgrove Health NHS Trust, and a minor royal. From the look of almost orgasmic rapture on his humpty dumpty bonce, Sidney clearly felt he had scaled the social Himalayas.

Noakes had got it in one. Or perhaps that should be a hole-in-one, the DI thought as a wave of almost hysterical levity threatened his composure.

The head honcho at the Trust was Sidney's new BF. Probably the two of them were firm golfing buddies to boot. No way was the DCI going to let Markham spoil the party.

Damn and double damn.

Time to regroup.

Wearing his blandest expression, the DI said, 'Of course, sir, as you advised, we need to start with the Newman's patient population. In such a potentially dangerous environment, any number of psychological disorders could be implicated.'

The formula worked its magic. Sidney was lapping it up.

'Excellent. No stone unturned, Inspector,' he replied almost cordially, satisfied that Markham's tiresome tendency to insurrectionism had been subdued by superior force of arms. *So important for young officers to heed the voice of wisdom.*

Noakes was looking hard at him, but Markham gave an imperceptible shrug of the shoulders. *I'll tell you when we get out of here.*

Once they were clear of Miss Peabody – anxiously on the look-out for a change in weather fronts – Noakes turned to the

DI accusingly. 'You didn't tell him owt about that lobotomy stuff.' He bent his shrewd gaze on Markham. 'Nor bent coppers neither.'

'I could see there was nothing doing, Noakesy. Keep out signs all over the shop.'

'Yeah?'

'There was a new picture of Sidney pressing the flesh with the CEO of the Health Trust ... I think Ted Cartwright was oiling away in the background, but wasn't close enough to see.'

'Ah,' Noakes said in a tone of deep comprehension. 'Now I'm with you, Guv.'

'We were too deep in bushy haired stranger territory ... anything about malpractice or corruption was doomed to fall on deaf ears.'

'You should wheel in Burton next time, Guv. Get her to bring all them psychology textbooks ... Sidney'd love it. They could have a cuppa an' a nice cosy chat about Ted Bundy an' all the other freaks.'

Markham grinned mischievously. 'It just so happens the DCI read psychology at university like Kate.'

'I might've bloody guessed.'

'I saw a few titles by Paul Britton and David Canter on the DCI's bookshelves, so I fancy he's interested in criminal profiling and the like.'

'Oh aye.' Noakes sounded profoundly unimpressed. 'Thinks he's chuffing Cracker like as not.'

Markham squared his shoulders. 'We'll have to humour him. Let's just be thankful he didn't say anything about a press conference.' Suddenly exhaustion slammed into him like a truck. 'Look, Noakesy, see if you can put a rocket under Ted Cartwright. I want those records. Then check in with Kate and Doyle. See where they're up to on patient and staff movements.'

'Those sodding spreadsheets,' the DS growled.

'Yes, can't be helped I'm afraid. Kate can also rustle up some clinical data for the in-patients ... that way at least we can blind Sidney with science while seeing where the psychosurgery angle takes us. Then there's—'

'You get off,' Noakes cut in. Slyly he added, 'Reckon I know what you need, Guv.'

'Oh yes, what's that?'

'Coupla bouts down at Doggie Dickerson's.' The DS alluded to the gym in Marsh Lane where Bromgrove Police Boxing Club had its unofficial headquarters. Little more than three dingy rings plus sanitary installations of dubious hygienic integrity, this was Markham's invariable antidote to encounters with the DCI.

'You've read my mind, Sergeant,' the DI replied. 'Tell the others, briefing 7 a.m. sharp tomorrow.'

As the DI entered the decrepit premises, Doggie shambled out to meet him, a distinct aroma of whisky following in his wake.

God, thought Markham, the old rogue looks more disreputable than ever. A dead ringer for Fagin or some other Dickensian villain.

Doggie's was a favourite haunt of Bromgrove CID and the local criminal fraternity alike. Under its dodgy auspices, there existed a kind of brotherhood between hunter and hunted, professional hostilities being suspended while they beat the proverbial seven bells out of each other in the ring. For all its seediness, the rough authenticity of the place exactly suited Markham. Far more so than the antiseptic atmosphere of more conventional gyms.

His grey wig wildly askew, Doggie greeted his 'fav'rite 'spector' with unusual condescension and affability, in the process disclosing more of his yellow-toothed orthodontics than Markham cared to behold on a full stomach.

"Lo, Mr Markham.'

'How goes it, Doggie?'

'Can't complain, Mr Markham. Your Mr Carstairs was in earlier, givin' it some welly.'

Like Markham, Chris Carstairs from Vice derived similar therapeutic benefits from a sweaty slug-fest. On this occasion, the DI was not sorry to have missed him. Wrung out from Sidney, it would be more than he could take.

Doggie measured his man with a shrewd eye.

'C'mon, Mr Markham, I'll 'ave the right partner ready for you in a jiffy.'

The DI turned towards the euphemistically entitled locker room. A thought struck him. 'You were a professional, Doggie.' In another life.

'Oh aye,' was the laconic response.

'Did you ever see boxers with brain injuries?'

'I've seen plenty o' pasta brains in my time, Mr Markham. Blokes turned to mush. Nothin' left. But,' Doggie shook his head sadly, the wig wobbling from side to side, 'nobody wanted to talk about it. Bad for business y'see.' And with that, he shuffled away.

Turned to mush. Nothing left. Bad for business.

Those phrases echoed in Markham's mind as he swung at his bull-like opponent, imagining that he was giving Sidney a pasting – *Take that, you bastard. And that!* – and they continued to reverberate as he headed for home. More and more, he was inclined to think that delving into the shadowy world of psychosurgery – that bourne from which human beings returned only as wrecks – was likely to be bad for business. The question was, whose?

*

'I remember the Hewitt case, Gil. That poor woman was virtually decapitated in front of her three children ... all under ten. Wasn't there a misdiagnosis by some psychiatrist at the Newman?'

'Yes, it was Doctor Warr whose body's just turned up in Bromgrove Woods.'

Olivia looked startled. 'He took a drubbing in the press, but got off the hook in the end.'

'That's right.' Markham made a sound somewhere between disgust and laughter. 'The Trust called in the big guns ... basically, they chucked around enough clinical labels – mixed affective state, bipolar disorder, blah blah – to ensure he got the benefit of the doubt.'

'Throwing sand in people's eyes.'

'Precisely.'

Markham looked lovingly across the table. After the bleached and double-bleached brightness of the Newman – all those endlessly shiny reflective surfaces – the dim cosiness of their living room, curtains drawn tight against the misty night, fell upon him like balm.

Supper over, they pulled their armchairs up to the wood-burning stove in the fireplace.

'D'you think Dr Warr made other mistakes, Gil?' Olivia asked, burrowing into the depths of her chair with a girlish snuggle. With her waterfall of red hair, pallor and long slender fingers, she looked more than ever like one of those sirens of legend who lured men to their doom.

'Warr wouldn't be the first doctor to have a messiah complex.' Markham's eyes were shadowed. 'The fact that he had friends in high places helped him ... experts were falling over themselves to say it might not have been schizophrenia and there was a reasonable difference of medical opinion.'

'Like the Yorkshire Ripper and the voices telling him to kill prostitutes,' Olivia said thoughtfully. 'You remember, Gil, they said he wasn't mad at his trial, so he went to prison. Then later he ended up in Broadmoor after they decided he was a paranoid schizophrenic—'

'And now he's back in prison again on the basis that he's not mentally ill any more,' Markham concluded for her. 'All round the houses because the so-called experts can't agree.' He gave an exasperated sigh. 'You couldn't make it up!'

'I suppose doctors will always come up smelling of roses because they stick together.'

'Well, hopefully the White Coat Effect isn't as potent as it used to be, sweetheart.'

Grey-green eyes regarded him earnestly.

'There's been another one, hasn't there?' she said softly. 'Another murder.'

Haltingly, Markham told her about Hayley – from their first encounter with the chirpy little receptionist to the discovery of her remains concertinaed in the freight elevator.

'Poor George.' Olivia's eyes were over-bright. 'She'd be about the same age as his daughter. It must have been shattering for him.'

Markham had never quite fathomed the psychic affinity between his ethereal girlfriend and the lumbering subordinate who put backs up wherever he went. But Noakes was as devoted to her as any medieval troubadour to his mistress, much to the irritation of Mrs Noakes who was wont to declare that her husband was 'bewitched'. Equally impervious to his wife's tart asides and the ribbing of colleagues, Noakes's enthralment never wavered. As though this secret passion represented the poetry of his sergeant's existence, Markham half suspected he would be content to make a figure before Olivia and expire in a haze of chivalric bliss. Now he said quietly, 'I'm ashamed I forgot about that, Liv. You're right, it must have hit Noakes hard.'

To lighten the mood, he recounted the meeting with Slimy Sid.

'God, that man's a real weasel,' she said feelingly. 'I don't know how you manage not to punch his lights out.'

'I went to Doggie Dickerson's straight afterwards.' Markham grinned.

Olivia chuckled. 'Good for you, love. The DCI'll never know how much he owes Doggie.'

They sat companionably, savouring the other's nearness.

'So, you're going to run a dummy investigation for Sidney while secretly doing your own thing.'

'Yes.'

He hesitated, torn between the desire to keep their home life untainted by his work and the need to unburden himself.

'Go on, Gil. It's all right.'

'There's an ongoing investigation into malpractice at the Newman.'

'Oh yes, I remember seeing something in the *Gazette* about it.'

'The DCC's asked me to look into something potentially a great deal more sinister ... patients who went into the Newman and never came out.'

'As in they died there,' Olivia said faintly.

'As in they vanished ... no death certificate ... nobody appearing to know their whereabouts.'

'You mean they've just *gone*?' His girlfriend looked at him in horror. 'But *how*?'

'That's what I need to find out,' Markham said grimly. 'Doctor Warr was involved in psychosurgery – lobotomies – in the past. The answer may lie there.'

'I've heard of that.' Olivia sounded both repelled and fascinated. 'It's when they cut into fibres at the front of the brain … .to reduce the sex drive and make women more manageable.'

Markham was surprised. 'Well, not just women.'

Scarlet spots burned on his girlfriend's pale cheeks and she gave a queer little laugh. Then she looked at Markham remorsefully, slipping down on the rug beside his chair and laying her head on his arm. 'I should have told you, Gil. I'm thinking of signing up for out-patient therapy at the Newman. Leslie who runs the Women's Group at the university reckons it'd be a good idea.'

Markham felt disagreeably jarred but did his best not to show it. He knew there was something in Olivia's past that she hadn't yet shared with him. He had told himself that it didn't matter, that he had his own secrets, that she would tell him when she was ready. But increasingly he had begun to wonder if the time would ever come.

Suddenly, there came into his mind the image of Anna Sladen and the way her clear blue eyes had looked at him. The spirit of the sea personified.

Just as quickly, the image was gone.

He felt a pang of compunction, as though he had somehow been unfaithful.

Gently, he laid his hand on the tousled red head.

'Just stay safe, dearest.' He laughed ruefully. 'I can't wrap you in cotton wool, however much I might like to. But there's a killer at large.' Maybe two. 'The Newman is a dangerous place.'

'I'll be careful, scout's honour.'

Lightly, but with something of a creepy sensation in the region of her spine, Olivia swatted away his fears.

They began to talk of other things. The red embers glowed upon the hearth and the sense of furtive evil, watching from the shadows with hostile eyes, was gone.

7

Diminishing Returns

'Feeling better, Guv?'

Noakes looked sideways at Markham as the DI drove them to the Newman on Wednesday morning.

'Well, I worked off some of the aggro at Doggie's, that's for sure.'

He hoped the DS wouldn't notice that he hadn't given a straight answer.

In truth, he was feeling curiously unsettled. He had always thought of himself and Olivia as soulmates, so it hurt to know that there was an area of her life he couldn't enter or understand, and that she had erected some kind of cordon sanitaire aimed at keeping him out.

Part of him knew that his resentment was illogical and unfair. Having been abused by his stepfather in childhood while his mother looked the other way, Markham was apt to shrink from any contact with the hidden wound. Inwardly wrapping himself in iron-clad reserve, his famously austere professional persona kept the demons at bay. He knew what colleagues said. 'Markham's a cold bastard.' Yes, like ice, he thought grimly. You touch it and it burns you. Even with Noakes, whatever the DS may have guessed, the subject was never broached.

One of the reasons Markham fell in love with Olivia was her exquisite sensitivity – the fact that she never stooped to poke nor pry, but simply listened with generous sympathy to whatever he chose to share. He knew he ought to reciprocate in kind. But somehow he could not, and the awareness that there was an area of her life declared 'out of bounds' gnawed at him like a canker and marred the delight of their comradeship. At other times, he was almost able to forget. But increasingly he felt the hidden sting, sharp and insistent like a burr against his skin.

She was no longer his rose without a thorn ...

Summat's up, Noakes thought. The guvnor's got that bruised look round the eyes, but not from any punch thrown at Doggie's.

Olivia. Olivia.

All heaven opened before Noakes when he thought of the boss's girlfriend with her ethereal delicacy and look of another world. He never sought to know the source of this dumb reverence. He only knew that it was as much a part of him as the air he breathed.

Whatever was amiss, he'd be there. What did they call it? An honest broker. Well, that's what he'd be. A friend to them both.

Fortified by thoughts of the faithful service he meant to render, Noakes settled back for a quick snooze.

It was another misty morning, fog clinging to familiar landmarks which peered wraith-like through a grey veil. The vaporous light shrouded the Newman too, making the hospital seem to recede like a stage set behind a screen.

Markham felt a curious reluctance to go in.

As they sat looking at the building, sunlight suddenly glowed through the fog, turning its greyness crimson, like the throbbing blood-red thoughts of those confined inside.

Slowly, reluctantly, they headed to reception and another round of security checks.

Kate Burton was already at her post in the Incident Room. DC Doyle exchanged a long-suffering look with Noakes who winked as if to say, 'don't worry, lad, you can tell me all about it over a pint later.' On reflection, judging by the look on his colleague's face, several pints.

'The autopsy report on Hayley's through, sir.'

'And?'

'She was strangled.'

'Any sexual interference?'

'No, sir.'

'Unusual features?'

'None, sir.'

Suddenly Noakes spoke.

'Someone must've closed her eyes.'

'Your point, Sergeant?'

'Well, when we found her in that ... hatch thing...' For a moment the DS sounded choked, then he continued. 'It looked like the lass had been posed ... kinda like she was tucked up in bed. She had her eyes shut like she was sleeping ... like in a Disney film.... *Snow White* ...' His voice tailed off.

Markham remembered what Olivia had said about Noakes's daughter. He was the only parent in the team.

'Well observed, Noakesy,' he said warmly.

'So whoever killed Hayley could've felt bad about it ... could've *cared* about her in some twisted way ... is that what you're saying?' Burton looked longingly at her array of alienists' almanacs, visibly itching to look up *Modus Operandi: Signature, Staging and Posing.*

'Correct, Kate.'

'Not like what happened with Doctor Warr, then?'

'No,' replied Markham, thinking of the mutilation to which their first victim's corpse had been subjected.

The DI turned to DC Doyle. 'Where are we up to with staff and patients?'

The young DC's frank open face looked what Noakes would have called kerflummoxed.

'Don't worry, Detective,' the DI said hastily as he reached for a pile of spreadsheets. 'The abridged version's fine.'

'Well, it looks as though everyone was where they were supposed to be. None of the patients off the wards or anything like that.'

'Any chance the security systems could've been bypassed?'

'They're pretty much foolproof, sir. Claire Holder got the electronic geeks, er, facilities guys, to explain all the protocols. And we had the full tour, all the bells and whistles.' Bloody literally, he thought sourly. That was three hours of his life he'd never get back. And as for Burton, the silly cow behaved like all her Christmases had come at once. One frigging question after another.

'Fascinating,' the DI said coolly, leaving Doyle with the uneasy feeling that the guvnor had read his mind.

Markham turned to Burton. 'How about Ted Cartwright, Kate? Have those records come yet?'

'Faxed through earlier this morning, sir.'

'Right, I suppose that's something.' Markham began to pace up and down restlessly before catching himself up short. God, he was like one of those animals in captivity, weaving and circling, up and down, up and down. There must be some malignant germ in the air of the place which had infected his bloodstream.

Unobtrusively, he forced himself to breathe deeply.

'Okay, this is the drill. Noakes and I are going to pay a visit to the intensive care ward. I want to speak to Mikey Belcher ... hear what he's got to say about patients disappearing.'

Burton looked disappointed. Thank Christ the guvnor had ruled her out of the ward round, thought Noakes. If she started yakkety-yakking about 'isms' and the like, they'd get sweet FA out of Belcher.

'Kate, I'd like you and Doyle to get started in the archives room,' the DI said. 'Data checks on the names Cartwright's given us. Get that nice volunteer Linda Harelock to give you a hand. I don't know if there's an archivist, but Claire Holder should be able to find you some help.'

'That woman's an alkie,' Doyle said glumly. 'Always dashing off to "see to something",' he air quoted sardonically, 'then comes back smelling of extra strength mints.'

'She was having it away with the good doctor.'

The DC's eyebrows shot up. '*You're kidding me!*'

'That's pure supposition, Noakes,' Markham put in mildly. 'But it's true she was definitely overwrought when we talked to her about Doctor Warr.'

'David Belcher said Holder was up to summat with Warr, Guv.'

'Hearsay, Noakes. And remember, the man has an axe to grind against the hospital authorities for keeping him away from Mikey.'

But Markham was thoughtful. There had been something frightened, almost *furtive*, in Claire Holder's face and manner, as though she was hanging on by a thread.

'She spoke of Doctor Warr's dedication,' he said musingly. 'I wonder how much she knew about those ice pick operations and any extra-curricular research.'

'If there was some sort of cover-up, she could've been part of it.' Clearly, the conspiracy theory was gaining ground with Burton.

'Watch her, Kate ... unobtrusively, of course.'

Burton nodded vigorously.

'And keep her away from any data search.'

A little knowledge is a dangerous thing.

Having briefed the other two, Markham and Noakes headed off in the direction of the intensive care ward.

'I hate these scanners and air lock thingies,' Noakes muttered as he plodded along like a disgruntled shire horse.

'Be thankful for small mercies, Sergeant. In some places, we wouldn't be able to go anywhere without an escort. With this place being relatively small-scale and mostly medium secure, it's not so oppressive. Stabbuck House on the other side of Medway is a whole different ball game. More like a prison.'

The DS was clearly not much reassured by this philosophical response.

'Poor little Hayley was right impressed by it,' he said. 'Mebbe she was thinking about going in for nursing.' He looked wrathfully at the CCTV above their heads. 'What a fucking waste.'

Suddenly, Markham spotted the head porter Ernie Roberts trundling his trolley along the other side of the corridor while giving instructions to a spotty youth at his side.

'Morning, Mr Roberts,' he said cordially, hoping the encounter would jolt Noakes out of his ill humour. The spotty youth apparently had no appetite for conversation with the police, contenting himself with an awkward bob of the head before scuttling off.

Ernie smiled like a pleased child at the greeting, but close up the DI noticed a curiously lost expression in his eyes and an irresolute trembling of the lips. Although the porter looked like the kind of man to dread most women, Markham remembered Linda Harelock having mentioned that he was close to the murdered girl. Her death must have knocked him sideways, especially following so close on the grisly discovery in Bromgrove Woods.

Noakes too noticed how strangely drawn and grey the man looked.

'How're you bearing up, Mr Roberts?'

'Work's the best medicine for me, sir.' But the shaking hands told another story.

'Ex-army, ain'tcha?' the DS enquired respectfully.

'That's right, sir. South Lancashire.'

The shy face was aglow with pleasure.

'You can allus tell. Youngsters'll make a ruddy fuss, but your mob just get on with the job.'

Under Noakes's approving gaze, the ungainly stooping figure seemed to grow three inches.

With a smart little salute, the porter smiled at them and went on his way.

'Sound fella that.'

Markham suppressed a smile. That was Noakes. Beneath the cantankerous, crusty exterior, he understood the language of the heart. Perhaps that was why he and Olivia were fast friends before a word had passed between them.

Shortly, they found themselves in the passage which led to the forensic unit.

Noakes's apprehension had returned.

'Gives me the creeps big time,' he growled. 'All this happy-clappy artwork.' He gestured to the over bright seaside paintings. 'Then once you get through there, it's those big steel doors with peepholes. Jus' like *One Flew Over The Cuckoo's Nest.*'

'Well, do your best to stay relaxed, Noakes,' Markham said absently, his mind running on the photograph that had vanished from the wall between their first and second visits to the corridor. The one with the sinister little villas like desolate hives in a lonely landscape. The one signed with the words *Your Friend.*

Did Hayley think she was meeting a friend when she went to her death?

Did she realize too late that she had backed herself into a corner?

Did she scream and struggle and fight for her life...?

'You coming or what?' Noakes wanted to get it over.

The intensive care ward was as much like an underwater tank as ever.

Markham felt as though they were moving in slow motion.

He noticed that Noakes averted his eyes from the heavy-duty steel doors which marked off the living quarters of the most dangerously disturbed. It was true, he thought, the sight of them possessed a quality to freeze the blood.

This forbidding impression was momentarily dispelled when Doctor Lopez came towards them, toothpaste smile bright against the dark complexion, his vitality in marked contrast to the various vacant-eyed figures who shuffled dog-like around the nursing station.

The DI couldn't decide if he liked him or not. A stocky middle-aged woman introduced as Sister Appleton clearly resented their presence on the ward, but the young consultant seemed unfazed. It probably helped that Claire Holder had not accompanied them.

'Let me take you to Mikey,' he said, leading the two men to the primrose-coloured recreation area. 'I would ask you not to say anything about the murders. For obvious reasons, we haven't shared that information with service users.'

David Belcher's brother sat in an easy chair at the far end of the room, his gaze resting listlessly on a little group of patients and staff playing cards at one of the pine tables which ran along the walls. Short, dark and scrawny, he had the compact build of a boxer. Bantamweight, thought Markham, visualizing his sparring partners at Doggie's.

But, for all that his wiry frame hinted at power, there was something defeated and hopeless about him, as though some inner spark had been quenched, snuffed out by experiences far beyond the visitors' power to comprehend.

Compassion flared in Noakes's eyes.

'Okay if we sit down, mate?'

'Be my guest.' Softly spoken, like his brother, there was the faint trace of a northern accent.

'How about a cuppa?' the DS said. 'Mine's white with three sugars, luv.' He smiled beatifically at Sister Appleton, ignoring the way she bristled at her demotion to tea lady.

Mikey smiled. It was the first real sign of animation he had shown.

'There's some vending machines round the corner,' he said. 'Next to the therapy room.'

'We'll do the honours,' Doctor Lopez said with a meaning-ful glance at his colleague who simpered in a way that turned Markham's stomach.

'She didn't like that,' Mikey said once they were dispatched on their errand.

'I know,' returned Noakes happily.

The simple exchange broke the tension, as though Mikey had recognized a kindred spirit in the stumpy sergeant.

They chatted about everyday things, the policemen touched by how hard the patient tried to find conversation, to somehow make his situation appear normal. When Doctor Lopez and Sister Appleton rejoined them and made as if to sit down, Mikey seemed to shrink inside his baggy jacket.

'Marvellous,' the DI said heartily. 'Right, I think we can take it from here, thank you.'

The indignant protest on Sister Appleton's lips subsided before Markham's coolly authoritative stare, while Doctor Lopez – after the briefest hesitation – nodded. 'We won't be far away.'

Setting down the refreshments on an adjacent coffee table, they promptly withdrew, though the nurse continued to hover at the far end of the lounge.

Mikey's exhausted eyes rested on his visitors with gratitude.

'Reckon it must be a relief to have a break from the medicos now an' again,' Noakes observed, staring after Doctor Lopez's retreating back with no very benignant expression.

'Ain't that the truth,' sighed the other.

'Are they treating you all right in here, Mr Belcher?' Markham asked. And then, as the patient's eyes flickered sideways, 'Don't be afraid, whatever you tell us is confidential. Just between the three of us, I promise.'

'We won't be sharing it with Dr Kildare over there,' growled Noakes, reaching for his tea.

'Look, I know I'm a sick man, gents... I crossed the line ... did bad things which landed me here.... Lashed out at staff as well cos ... well ... they weren't always kind and I've got a temper.'

'We know you had it rough growing up.'

'So did Dave.' His face suddenly looked tiny and vulnerable. 'I couldn't keep him safe,' he whispered. 'You can't imagine how terrible that was.'

For one searing moment, Markham saw the face of the little brother he couldn't protect, long since lost to drink and drugs. *Yes, I can,* he thought.

'Up till now they said I was doing well ... almost ready to move on from high dependency...'

'An' then you blew it?' Noakes was elaborately casual. 'Didn't do enough sucking up?'

Mikey grinned and some of the strain seemed to leave his face.

Well done, Noakesy.

'Rick and Tony, two of my mates ... they've been in here longer than anyone else.... They told some story in the patients' council about women going missing from the hospital years ago ... said they'd gone to be cut up and never came back.' He looked at them helplessly. 'They're a bit bonkers and it sounded very Boris Karloff, so I couldn't tell if they were taking the piss.' With a shaky smile he continued. 'But it bothered me.... Kept me awake at nights.... They said it was Doctor Warr and a policeman who took care of things ... called him Magnum.'

'You reported this?' Markham's voice was sharp.

'Yeah ... for all the good it did me.'

'Go on.'

'The guys said they were just showing off – trying to freak the rest of us out with ghost stories and stuff. Doctor Lopez and the rest of them told me to drop it.' Mikey's eyes flashed scorn, and he suddenly appeared much more alert than the apathetic figure they had initially encountered. 'But it didn't feel like a ghost story, Inspector. And there was something about the way they looked – all sly and knowing. I just *knew* they were telling the truth.'

'What happened after that?'

'Well, everybody shut up about it ... except me ... I s'pose I got angry when people wouldn't listen, which didn't help.'

'How did you get on with Doctor Warr?'

Mikey looked surprised. If this was a performance he was acting, he was the best actor Markham had ever seen.

'I didn't like him.' The dark brows knitted. 'It felt like he was always trying new things out on me ... that I was just a guinea pig. After he left and Miss Sladen took over it was much better.' There was a faint sparkle in his eyes now, a gleam of hope. 'She's going to arrange for me to see Dave again.'

'Good,' said Markham, not caring to analyze the odd, newly awakened consciousness he felt at hearing the attractive psychologist's name. 'There's no reason why you shouldn't be able to have visits.'

'Unless you wig out,' put in Noakes laconically.

Markham sighed theatrically. 'You must forgive my sergeant's lack of bedside manner, Mr Belcher.'

Mikey gave a bark of laughter.

Sister Appleton's head whipped round in the direction of the sound.

'Bandits at six o'clock,' Noakes said out of the side of his mouth as she came towards them.

They got to their feet.

Mikey extended his hand. 'Thanks for listening,' he said simply.

The nurse looked suspiciously at them as though this was an act of dangerous freemasonry.

Escorting them past the goldfish bowl nursing station in its perspex bubble, she said abruptly, 'Far be it from me to interfere.'

In Markham's experience, this was invariably the preface to people making him a present of their opinion.

'But,' here it comes, he thought, 'the patients on this ward are highly manipulative.' Sister Appleton's lips tightened. 'Pathologically deceptive and highly impulsive. You shouldn't take them at face value.'

That's us told, then.

Doctor Lopez was nowhere to be seen. Markham wondered if he had hightailed it to Claire Holder's office to brief her on their proceedings.

'Thanks for your input, Sister Appleton,' he said crisply. 'I understand from Mr Belcher that his visitation rights are going to be restored in the near future.' He gave her a long hard stare. 'You can be assured, I am taking a close personal interest in his case.'

'Ta, luv,' Noakes said with sunny innocence. 'It's not so bad in here. Quite cosy akshually.' He looked around wide-eyed. 'Bit like a youth club.' He winked at her. 'If you don't count the padded cells.'

The woman crimsoned to her hairline. Before Noakes could utter another word, the DI propelled him firmly through the swing doors and out into the corridor.

'God, Sergeant,' he said, 'no point winding them up unnecessarily. Cooperation's the name of the game, remember.'

'Her and Doctor Lopez ... a right smarmy pair ... gave me the willies, both of 'em.'

'I didn't much care for them myself,' Markham admitted. 'And it sounds like Mikey was on to something. But let's not jump to any conclusions. The patients back there are on that ward because they've done some pretty terrible things ... too dangerous for release into the community.' The DI looked apprehensively along the linoleum-floored corridor as though the walls could hear his words. Lowering his voice, he said, 'We can't rule anyone out.'

Noakes nodded phlegmatically.

'Where to now, boss?'

'Let's see how they're getting on with the archives.'

The archives room was as thoroughly claustrophobic as the rest of the hospital, despite being situated in the old heart of the building. A window at the back looked out on to a shrubbery. In summer, the sun-dappled copse no doubt afforded an inviting retreat, but on a dank winter morning its dark, cavernous bushes looked menacing as though the rustling undergrowth might conceal who knew what horrors.

Markham gave himself an admonishment not to be morbid. It was just the contrast between the new buildings' toy-town brilliance and the crumbling gloom of the Victorian architecture that he found unsettling.

Burton and Doyle were hunched over the index card cabinets. Beside them, Linda Harelock studied the paperwork that had been faxed through from Ted Cartwright's office with frowning concentration, her pleasant face the picture of honest bewilderment.

'I take it none of those names mean anything to you, Mrs Harelock?'

'I'm racking my brains, Inspector, but it's just a fog,' she said apologetically. 'If we can pin them to something in the files, maybe I'll have a better idea.'

'We're talking the eighties and nineties, sir,' Burton piped up.

'Oh, that was when Doctor Kennedy was here.' Linda Harelock was glad to contribute something.

'Doctor Kennedy?'

'He's dead now, him and Doctor Molloy. They were Doctor Warr's mentors when he was training.'

Markham jammed his hands into his pockets.

Dead. And their secrets buried with them, no doubt.

'Isn't there some sort of computer database of patients?' he asked in exasperation. 'I mean, isn't there a system for cross-referencing?'

'Not for that time frame, sir.' Burton pulled a face. 'Nothing for it but to go through the boxes.' She gestured wearily at the shelving and stacks.

The DI thought of that confidential file back on his desk at the station. From the sound of it, Cartwright had only sent over the cold cases, but the DCC wanted answers for patients who had fallen off the radar in the last five years.

He needed to check the more recent cases. There was bound to be some sort of computer trail he could follow. *Had to be.*

If some past conspiracy lay behind Jonathan Warr's murder, then its tentacles reached into the present....

He swung round to Noakes. 'I want to speak to Mr Hewitt. He lost his wife through Doctor Warr's flawed clinical judgment, so I figure he's worth a visit. Then I want to run some checks back at the station.'

'Righto, Guv.'

Outside, a sullen mackerel sky brooded overhead.

The smooth, clean curves of the Newman's modern wings snaked out from the old Victorian tower with its hanging clock.

Time was running out.

8

Wheels Within Wheels

JIM HEWITT LIVED A little way outside Bromgrove in the suburb of Riversdale, so there was time to mull over developments.

'Doctor Warr was sixty-four when he was murdered.' Markham ran through the scenario out loud. 'That means he would have been in his mid-thirties and forties when he was working under those other two doctors ... Kennedy and Molloy....'

'Climbing the greasy pole, Guv,' Noakes agreed. 'So, if they were doing dodgy operations, he could've been in on it.'

'Lobotomies had their heyday in the nineteen-forties and fifties,' the DI mused. 'Once tranquilizers came along, there wasn't the same need for invasive surgery.'

'No more poking around in folks' skulls, then.' Noakes sounded relieved.

'Well, it's much subtler now. You won't find doctors cracking through the orbital bone with an ice pick. These days it's all computer-guided electrodes and precision technology – like when people have keyhole surgery.' Markham grimaced. 'Supposedly, none of it can be done without the patient's consent, but …'

'If there was no messy stuff involved in the ops, then why'd the killer stab Warr through the eye?'

'I've been thinking about that.' Markham negotiated a tricky roundabout before resuming. 'Doctor Warr had an antiquarian's interest in medicine. That office of his was wall to wall histories of neurology, including the glory days of the lobotomy…. There was a whole shelf devoted to ice pick surgery…. Made me wonder if our murderer shared Warr's fascination….'

'What, they sat in his room looking up gory details?'

'Something like that, yes…. Becoming fixated and brooding.'

'S'pose it's possible,' Noakes conceded. 'His room wasn't cordoned off or owt like that, so chummy could've snuck in … assuming they got one of those swipe card thingies for the door.' The DS scowled ferociously, as was his habit when following a train of thought. 'So, you're saying the killer decided those dead medicos an' Warr fucked about with someone … a relative or someone they loved … an' plotted to get revenge?'

'If by "fucked about" you mean the doctors reduced their patient to the condition of a zombie, with no personality or independent will, then yes, I think that's what had happened. Kennedy and Molloy were beyond our murderer's reach—'

'Which left Warr.'

'Exactly.'

'Jesus.'

It was an uncomfortable image. The murderer, incubating and feeding that hatred, as though the Newman was some monstrous hatchery.

'Why would someone end up getting operated on like that?'

'Oh, there could be any number of reasons.' After Olivia had gone to bed the previous evening, Markham had sat at the computer in his study reading everything he could find about psychosurgery and the abuses it had spawned. 'Mental retar-dation, depression, hypersexuality, schizophrenia, alcoholism. Or maybe,' Markham's expression was grim, 'the possession of money when others wanted it.'

'Blimey.'

They drove in silence for a little while, watching as the town gave way to fields and bridle paths, still with that leaden sky draining colour from the landscape, smudging it with a ghostly sfumato.

'Why not jus' drug 'em?' Noakes enquired finally. 'Zonk 'em out with tablets.'

'Maybe a "final solution" was required – something that would erase any active thinking. End of story. Case closed.'

Noakes thought for a moment. 'Yeah, I c'n see the logic. With medication, it's allus got to be reviewed. There's prescriptions an' things…. An' pills ain't foolproof.'

Foolproof.

Before the DI's mind rose the haunting image of lobotomized subjects. Reduced to imbecility, their intellect severely limited by the surgery – like children, eternally destined to be five or six years old. But in reality, not children at all; often tall hulking figures of emotional complexity far beyond whatever formal intelligence was left with them, harbouring the remnants of impulses and passions that the surgeons' knives had not totally excised.

Noakes was coming around to the DI's theory. 'Yeah, an op takes care of everything,' he concluded. 'After that, you c'n jus' stick 'em in a home, somewhere out of the way.'

A home.

Villas. Cottages. Chalets.

Spirited away from the world. Gone from family letters, gone from family discussions, gone from family business. Gone.

Markham shuddered. What might it do to a human being to learn that a loved one had met such a fate?

These deeds must not be thought After these ways. So, it will make us mad.

'You all right, Guv?'

'Someone walking over my grave.'

'Oh aye,' Noakes grunted. 'Let's hope it's not an omen.'

'Cheers, Sergeant, that makes me feel a whole lot better.'

Jim Hewitt's was the last in a row of shabby cottages at the edge of Riversdale Common.

The place had a neglected, unloved air and Hewitt looked equally wretched, though he was neatly dressed, while the front room was tidy if cheerless with none of the knick-knacks, photos or personal touches which make a house a home. There was no sign of anyone else around. Presumably the children were at school or college.

Having politely offered tea, he disappeared into the kitchen to make it, returning minutes later with a tray which bore not only cups and saucers but a plate of biscuits.

After the briefest of hesitations, Noakes tucked in. Seeing as the bloke had made an effort, it'd be rude not to.

Hewitt's was an interesting face, the DI thought. So concave, it looked as though two profiles had been pressed together. Face and body were alike, very thin, possibly from the effect of some wasting fire within him, which found a vent in his sunken eyes.

'You're here about Doctor Warr.' He talked flatly, with no light and shade in his voice, yet his face grew sharper and paler. 'I'm glad he's dead,' he said simply, 'but I didn't kill him.'

Markham suddenly felt a surge of pity for Hewitt's children, living with this wreck of a human being.

'Did you have any contact with Doctor Warr after the

inquiry?' he asked gently.

'He never apologized, you know.' Hewitt ignored the question. 'Not a word of regret. Nothing. The arrogance was unbelievable. That's what really got me. The fact that he and the other so-called experts saw themselves as superior beings.... Warr even referred to Mary's death as collateral damage.' Then he seemed to register Markham's query. 'No, I didn't have anything to do with him ... or anyone else for that matter. I was like an untouchable. People crossed the road to avoid me – as if they thought they might catch something.' There was an unmistakable note of bitterness in his voice as he added, 'You find out who your friends are all right. Only that mental health campaigner gave me the time of day.' There was something dreadfully worn about the man's face as he looked back down the years. 'I never got near Warr,' he concluded. 'The hospital saw to that. Better protected than royalty, he was. But he didn't escape in the end.'

Then Hewitt smiled a slow smile. There was something about it that made Markham feel very uneasy, that gave him goose bumps. Even Noakes paused, a digestive halfway to his mouth.

Markham felt an overwhelming urge to be away from Jim Hewitt and out of his presence. He could tell his subordinate felt the same.

Five minutes later, they were in the car heading back to Bromgrove.

'Poor sod,' Noakes said. 'No wonder he's gone round the twist.'

'Just how twisted is he, Sergeant, that's the question. Twisted enough to kill?'

'Didn't look as if he had it in him, Guv. An' there was no reaction when you mentioned Hayley's name.'

'Appearances can be deceptive, Noakes.' Markham's fingers drummed on the steering wheel. 'And he admitted knowing David Belcher.'

Noakes grunted.

'Sounds like Warr thought he was God almighty, Guv.'

'Yes, that was interesting. Playing with people's lives.'

As though they were pawns on a chess set.

'What now, boss?'

'Back to CID. You can run some checks on Kennedy and Molloy while I take a look at the DCC's file and call in some favours at the CQC.' Before Noakes could ask 'Wassat?' Markham swiftly translated, 'The Care Quality Commission.'

'What about DCI Sidney?'

'I happen to know that the DCI is attending an Excellence in Policing conference in London today, Sergeant.' Markham grinned. 'So at least we'll be unmolested.'

'Any chance of—'

'A pit stop?'

'You took the words right out of my mouth, Guv.' With an air of long-suffering virtue, Noakes added, 'No elevenses, see ... I mean, Hewitt don't count.'

Deadpan, the DI replied, 'I could see it put you right off your food, Sergeant.'

The DS looked at Markham suspiciously, but could detect no sarcastic undertone.

'There's a Gregg's just past the next roundabout, Noakes, if that'll do you.'

'Champion.'

'But I warn you, after the grease-fest, it's all systems go.'

Markham felt a sudden sense of urgency, a flicker of the strange presentiment he often had when death or disaster was near. It was a specialized awareness that had been with him for as long as he could remember and had done him no favours in his early career. Eventually, he had learned to keep his psychic intuitions to himself.

'What is it, boss?' For all his earth-bound cloddishness, Noakes was always attuned to the DI's inner vibrations. It was one of the enduring mysteries of their partnership.

'I don't rightly know, Noakesy. Just a feeling about the Newman ... that we need to get over there.' Bracingly, he added, 'You can chow down on the way back to the station. Once we've done those checks, it's back to the hospital. Hopefully Kate and Doyle will have some intel for us by now.'

CID was blissfully quiet. No doubt his colleagues were taking full advantage of Slimy Sid's absence, thought Markham. While the cat's away....

Noakes disappeared into the outer office while the DI holed up in his room, impatiently sweeping a pile of overtime paper-work out of sight.

Time to hit the phones....

Fifty minutes later, the two men regarded each other glumly across Markham's desk. Outside, it was already growing dark, the last dregs of daylight fading imperceptibly into monochrome shades of grey. The regiment of leylandii which screened the police station from Bromgrove High Street tossed agitatedly as though they too were dissatisfied and restless.

'Anything on Kennedy and Molloy?'

'Nothing doing, Guv.' Noakes's frustration was palpable. 'At least, nowt that anyone'll admit to.' He sighed gustily. 'Hewitt was right about one thing. They all close ranks at the first whiff of trouble.'

'Nothing on their records? No warnings or reprimands?'

'Well, if there was anything, it ain't there now.' The DS

looked troubled. 'Reading between the lines, I'd say there were some major balls-ups early on, Guv…. I mean, they sounded like some kind of circus act … didn't seem to matter that some folk ended up cabbages when things didn't work out.'

Markham closed his eyes. 'Collateral damage.'

'Yeah. Warr must've felt right at home with Barnum and Bailey … the three of 'em could probably talk anyone into anything.'

'This was all pre-Shipman, of course,' Markham murmured. 'Rogue doctors are a rare breed nowadays.'

Noakes looked far from convinced. Then his hangdog features brightened momentarily. 'Kennedy's obituary says patients at the Newman called him their friend.' Noakes shuddered. 'Poor devils. Butcher, more like.' He delved into his jacket pocket and produced a crumpled photocopy. 'That's a picture of him and Molloy at some knees up.'

Markham wasn't sure what he had expected, but it certainly wasn't this.

They were perfectly ordinary. Nondescript. Two balding, stale, middle-aged men.

His sixth sense was dormant. He felt nothing at all….

'How'd you get on, Guv?'

'Not much better, Sergeant. I traced those five names the DCC gave me as far as the Newman. In each case, the patient was admitted for short-stay treatment but later placed on a section and detained involuntarily.'

'So, they couldn't leave … like prison.' Noakes's brow was furrowed as he processed this information. 'Who did the section?'

'Well, it needed two doctors plus another mental health professional – like a social worker.'

'Kosher?'

'Who can say … any small fry will have done whatever the doctors told them.'

'Signed on the dotted line.'

'Precisely.'

'What happened after that?'

'Patients were apparently transferred to the intensive care ward and then to a place called Seaview…. Only no-one seems sure where that is.'

'How could they send them somewhere that doesn't exist?' Noakes was nonplussed.

'Well, there *is* a rehabilitation centre of that name. On the outskirts of Brighton. The paperwork for the patients' transfer has the Brighton address. But they were never checked in there and the centre has no record of them ever being admitted.'

'Won't the ambulance service have a docket or summat?' the DS persisted doggedly. 'I mean, wouldn't they sort the transport and whatnot?'

Markham shook his head. 'They're denying all knowledge.'

'Jesus, Mary and Joseph.' Noakes's voice rose an incredulous octave. 'You mean someone *kidnapped* them?'

'Or spirited them away … Yes, it looks like they went under the radar.'

'Didn't the relatives kick up a stink?'

'This is where it gets interesting. In each case, power of attorney had been granted to a member of the immediate family prior to the section.'

'What's one of those?'

'Power of attorney allows someone else to make decisions if you become incapacitated.'

The light was dawning.

'Was there money sloshing around in these families?'

'Let's just say there weren't too many paupers on the list.'

Markham's voice was brittle.

'Chuffing Nora.' Noakes sagged in his chair.

'Indeed.'

'It was a regular racket then, Guv? Families an' medics in on it together?'

'Well, it looks like victims were chosen carefully. And not too many of them … the admissions to intensive care were well spaced out. Anything else would have aroused suspicion.'

The DI's lean handsome face was taut with concentration. 'Do you remember Hayley talking about how the Friends of the Newman raised funds to send patients on trips? Holiday chalets, she said.'

'Oh yeah.' A tender expression crossed Noakes's gnarled features at the thought of the receptionist. 'It was when we were looking at the weird photo of them funny little beach huts. *Hey*!' A thought struck him. 'D'you think that's where they stashed 'em, Guv?' The DS became very animated. 'Down at the seaside?'

'Yes,' Markham said slowly. 'That holiday complex was the perfect cover. Nice and remote. Safe from busybody interference.'

'An' the signature on the photo was *Your Friend*, remember, Guv? The same as Kennedy's creepy nickname.'

The DI smiled at his subordinate's excitement. Noakes had the bit between his teeth now.

'What happened to the patients in the end, boss? I mean, folk *can't* just vanish into thin air.'

The DI leaned forward intently. 'In the fifties and sixties, it would've been a cinch. If a family had the money and influence, they could literally *erase* the record and no-one would be any the wiser.'

'But what about later? What about *now*?' Noakes persisted

stubbornly, his beefy complexion mottled with consternation.

'Over time, given increased efficiency in the health service, it would have taken more skill to "disappear" someone.' Markham's lips were a thin line. 'But it could still be done, Sergeant. Technology was just getting started in the eighties and nineties ... which is why Kate and Doyle are scrabbling round in the archives at the hospital trying to get a handle on those names from Ted Cartwright.'

'What about the ones on the DCC's list?'

'According to Warr, they were eventually discharged back into the community.'

Noakes snorted.

'After that, apparently, they just walked out on their lives ... no contact with family ... fell through the net.'

'Didn't someone smell a rat?'

'Eventually, yes. In a couple of cases, friends and distant relations became suspicious – didn't buy the story. Words like "undue influence" and "coercion" were being bandied about.'

'How did Warr wriggle out of it?'

'It was easy enough to explain away Brighton. The hospital's holiday complex in Norfolk is called Seacrest, you see. So, all he had to do was claim there'd been a mix-up with the paperwork.'

'*Very* handy.'

Markham rubbed his temples distractedly. 'As for the dropping out scenario, it was child's play, Noakes. Social Care's like an overloaded electrical circuit ... can't cope with all the crises. You'd be surprised how many people go missing and are never seen again.'

'But these are *fruit loops* ... er, sorry, mental patients.'

'The appropriate terminology is "vulnerable disappeared", Sergeant. Oh, Missing Persons and the rest do their bit, but after a while ...' The DI's shrug was eloquent in its resignation.

'What d'you think happened, boss?' Noakes asked after a pause.

Markham's face was very sad.

He thought of those windswept Norfolk cottages.

'Neglect at best. Hastening the poor souls on their way at worst.'

'Like a serial killer?' The DS was appalled.

Markham gave a harsh laugh.

'Oh, I don't think Doctor Warr would have seen it in that light, Noakes. His apprenticeship with Kennedy and Molloy would have inured him to any pangs of conscience.' The DI recalled Jim Hewitt denouncing the doctor's arrogance. 'Saving families from pain and embarrassment is how he would have rationalized it to himself.'

'An' boosting his bank balance at the same time.'

'Fringe benefits,' Markham agreed sombrely, 'though I think the lure of illicit psychosurgery held considerable appeal for him.'

'Like one of them Nazi doctors.' Noakes was disgusted. 'I remember our Natalie did a project about 'em in school ... Dr Mangle or summat.'

The parallel with SS doctor Josef Mengele, the "God of Auschwitz" was horribly apt. And yet, for all his revulsion at the way Jonathan Warr had excised vulnerable individuals from their family annals, the DI told himself that the psychiatrist was himself a victim, indoctrinated and warped early in his career by those two bad angels....

'So the murderer's most likely connected to one of the poor daft buggers Warr an' the other two screwed over?'

'That's what I'm thinking.' Markham drew a deep breath. He seemed to be debating with himself. 'But I may have got it all wrong ... it could be something to do with the recent allegations about patient abuse.' His mouth set in a grim line. 'The good doctor's name has come up in that connection as well.'

'*Nah.*' The DS spoke in his most decisive tones. 'I reckon you're right, boss. Cutting him up an' that ... it's *got* to be linked with the surgery malarkey and mispers.'

A smile broke through the gloom of Markham's face.

'Thanks for the vote of confidence.'

'S'right.' Despite the studied casualness, it was clear Noakes was pleased.

'Who else knew what was going down, Guv?' Then, in a whisper, 'What about the Chief Super? Was *he* takin' a cut?'

Markham felt as though his head was going to explode.

Noticing how heavy the guvnor's eyes were, Noakes checked himself. From his pocket, he produced a Snickers bar. 'Get that down you, boss,' he said gruffly. 'You didn't have owt from Greggs.' A rosy glow travelling up his neck, he added, 'Your Olivia won't be happy if you conk out cos of not eating.'

Oddly enough, the cheap chocolate hit the spot.

Five minutes later, with Markham revived, the two men left the station on their way back to the hospital.

A blustery wind had got up while Markham and Noakes were thrashing out possible scenarios for murder.

The DI felt relief. As though something broke loose in him out of sympathy. Then the faintly mouldy coldness of the car park made him shiver, so he was glad after all of the warmth of the car.

In the Newman, Kate Burton was waiting for them. At the sight of her earnest face, Markham felt a pang of compunction. He should take her out with him more often. Give her a leg up what Noakes called the greasy pole.

'Any luck with the archives?'

'Well, we managed to track down index cards for the names, sir, but there's not much information save for the neurological jargon.'

Markham's compunction deepened as he spotted a copy of *Gray's Anatomy* at Burton's elbow.

Misinterpreting his look of concern, she said brightly, 'At least we know they were all psychosurgery patients here, sir. Doyle's running some computer checks, though given the dates it's probably a lost cause.'

'Good work, Kate.'

They were interrupted by Claire Holder.

'I need you, Inspector.' Her voice was hoarse, her face so white that the skilfully applied cosmetics stood out in patchy, streaky blotches like a clown's makeup.

Markham was already moving towards her.

'What is it, Ms Holder?'

'There's something blocking the ventilation shaft at the back of the clocktower.'

'Something?'

She moistened dry lips.

'One of the facilities team reported a noise earlier ... said it sounded like soot fall or rats. I went up to the viewing platform to check it out.... I'm the only one with access, you see.'

The woman swayed as though she was about to collapse.

Burton pressed her into a chair.

'Tell us what you saw, Ms Holder. And don't be afraid.' Markham was gentle but inexorable.

No words came.

'A body?'

His colleagues looked startled, but Markham was icy calm. All day, subconsciously, he had been thinking of death.

And now it had come again.

9

Aftermath

IT WAS A LONG way up to the viewing platform.

'Why can't we use the lift?' Noakes asked, pointing to a quaintly old-fashioned elevator to the left of a spiral stone staircase.

'That's just for show. An antique. It's rickety and temperamental, so we try to use it as little as possible.'

That's how the killer got his victim's body up to the top, Markham thought with a sudden searing conviction.

Markham, Noakes and Burton followed Claire Holder single file up the stairs which smelled unpleasantly dank and musty.

They emerged on to an expanse of black asphalt in the middle of which sat a circular concrete pod faced with glass panels.

At first, nobody spoke. It was strangely peaceful up on the roof, with a stiff breeze whipping their faces. After the claustrophobia of the oxygen-less hospital, Markham welcomed the eye-watering chill. Below them, the lights of the suburb gave off their neon phosphorescence, enveloping surrounding buildings in a lurid nimbus.

He turned to the director.

'You said you're the only one with access.'

'Well, it's a bit spooky up here, so staff give it a wide berth.' The woman gave a shaky laugh which teetered on the verge of hysteria. 'There was some nonsense about the ghost of a former patient who threw herself from the tower in Victorian times.' Attempting to sound more business-like, she added, 'This is the only key to the viewing deck.'

Easily nicked and copied. Noakes might as well have said it aloud.

Claire Holder was babbling now. '"Viewing deck" sounds a bit grand for what it is ... but you get a bird's eye view and some shelter ...'

And some privacy for the odd shag. Again, Noakes's expression was eloquent.

The director unlocked the door to the pod with shaking hands. At least, thought Markham, she'd had the wit to secure their crime scene.

Inside, it was very simple, just a concrete seat running round the wall.

In the centre of the floor, was a sunken oblong hatch covered with a wire mesh grille.

The DI squatted and squinted down through the grille before straightening up. With a lurch of her heart, Burton thought he looked as though he was standing at a graveside. Silently, she passed him a pocket torch.

'Thanks, Kate.'

Markham directed the flashlight down the shaft.

The other two both saw it then.

A glint of red.

Hair.

Wispy ginger hair.

They had found David Belcher's final resting place.

Noakes's face was working.

'Poor bugger,' he said. 'Him an' Mikey never even got that visit.'

'You know who it is?' The director sounded distracted.

Markham realized he had almost forgotten she was there. He nodded to Burton who took her by the arm.

'Let's go back down, Ms Holder. You were right, there's a body there, but we can't say anything more yet. I need to make some calls from your office.'

When they had gone, Noakes and Markham looked at each other.

Finally, the DI spoke.

'It was a stroke of bad luck for the murderer that something dislodged the body.' He knelt and loosened the grille which came away easily in his hands. 'It's about halfway down ... there's a bend in the pipe and he's lying over the curve.' Now Noakes too was squatting on his haunches, peering into the darkness below.

'What d'you reckon, Guv ... did they come up 'ere for a private word? Was he knocked out an' then shoved down the chimney? There's chemicals an' all sorts in there ... you'd be suffocated in no time.'

'I think he was more likely killed on the premises then brought up in that lift which was out of bounds, Sergeant.'

Noakes took this in. 'An' the moonshine about a ghost meant no-one'd be coming up for a shufti any time soon ... wonder who started *that* story...'

The two men rose to their feet and stood facing each other across the hatch.

Noakes jerked a thumb in the direction of the staircase.

'Her nibs was the only one who bothered with this place ... probl'y for a bit of how's your father with Warr.'

No-one got to the heart of the matter quite like the DS.

'It's likely they used this place for trysts, yes.' Markham murmured.

'*Yeah.*' Noakes was on a roll. 'Nice an' out of the way. Jus' the Shagnastys an' a bleeding ghost.... *Perfect*.... After Warr copped it, the killer could count on nobody paying a visit for yonks.' He shuddered. 'Any road, not till there was nobbut left of that poor lad but bones.'

Soberly, the DI nodded agreement.

'Mebbe chummy knew about Cruella de Vil's little visits an' wanted to pin it on her.'

'An added bonus, certainly.'

'Think she could've done it, Guv?' Noakes ducked his head awkwardly in the direction of the shaft. 'Yon fella didn't like her.' His underlip shot out. 'Hussy ... that's what 'e called her.'

'Harpy,' Markham amended mildly.

'Same difference.'

'We need to keep an open mind, Sergeant. She brought us up here, remember.'

'Could be a double bluff,' was the stubborn response.

'There's *something* she's not telling us,' Markham said thoughtfully, 'but that fear wasn't simulated.'

'Looked like she were going to puke her guts up, granted,' the DS conceded with lugubrious relish, 'but mebbe the reality was jus' sinking in ... mebbe shoving the lad down there was part of some sick ritual....'

The DI could see his subordinate was enraptured by the possibility of some occult or equally fantastic dimension. Time to administer a swift dose of reality.

'Next thing, you'll be telling me she's a practitioner of Wicca. Offering black masses up here with Doctor Lopez and Ernie Roberts!'

Noakes coloured, looking more than a little foolish as he returned to the sublunary sphere.

'Sorry, boss. I dunno,' he mumbled, 'there's summat about this place ...'

'It's okay. I feel it too.'

The DI looked at the sinister hatch. A trapdoor to hell.

We'll get the bastard, he promised David Belcher silently. We'll get whoever chucked you away like so much rubbish. And we'll finish what you started – force whatever lurks beneath this hospital's shiny blank surfaces into the light of day.

Noakes waited respectfully. He knew that funny closed look on the guvnor's face. It meant he was talking to the dead or summat. The missus called it 'Gilbert Markham's dreadfully *morbid* streak', but Olivia laughingly vowed that she and George (here the DS turned hot) would one day succeed in tearing her boyfriend from those vaults where he prowled taper in hand.

The DS didn't mind. He was used to it now. He hoped David Belcher could hear whatever the guvnor was saying.

'Right, Noakes.' The DI was ready to go. 'Backup should've arrived by now.'

They left the concrete chamber and moved across the asphalt towards the stairs.

The wind was rising, whistling more fiercely about the rooftop as though keening.

Lamentings heard in the air, strange screams of death.

But nothing would wake the sleeper in the shaft.

It took some time to sort the SOCOs, but at last they were dispatched to the observation platform with their arc lights and equipment, and quiet finally returned to the incident room.

The DI slumped into a chair.

'What did you do with Ms Holder, Kate?'

'Sent her home, sir. She'd only have got in the way. And besides, it looked like she was in shock. We'd not get any sense out of her tonight.' She hesitated. 'Was that right?'

'Absolutely. She'll keep till tomorrow.'

'I told her we needed CCTV footage for the last forty-eight hours, but – you're not going to like this, sir – it's been wiped.' She made a wry face. 'A blip, apparently.'

There was a despondent silence broken by Burton.

'What was Belcher *doing* here, sir? I mean, he hadn't been signed in at the front desk and nobody was aware of him being in the building.'

Except his murderer.

'How well did the staff know him?'

'I sent Doyle round the wards to check.' Burton flipped open her pocketbook. 'Doctor Lopez and Sister Appleton knew him from when he was allowed onto intensive care. Anna Sladen and a couple of the part-time psychologists had dealings when Mikey's care package changed and they took over from Doctor Warr.... Some of the nurses knew him from the campaign Behind Closed Doors ... a few of them were unhappy about all the negative PR.'

'Unhappy enough to kill?'

'Unlikely, sir. Doyle said they seemed genuinely shocked.'

'What about support staff – cleaners, housekeepers, facilities people?'

'Nothing doing, though one of the cleaners thought she remembered him from a few years back ... thinks he went to a couple of events organized by the volunteers, coffee mornings and what have you.'

'That ring any bells with Mrs Harelock? She's responsible for the befrienders, isn't she?'

'She said his face looked familiar, but she couldn't be sure if that was because she'd seen him at hospital events or because his face was in the *Gazette* a few times.'

Markham rubbed his five o'clock shadow ruminatively. It's not fair, thought Noakes. The rest of us look like shit, while the guvnor just gets better and better.

Oblivious of his sergeant's reflections on the cruel destiny which had endowed one of them with matinee idol good looks and the other a face only a mother could love, the DI continued quizzing Burton.

'Any of the porters clap eyes on him?'

'Nobody saw anything, sir, but ...' She consulted her notes. 'One of the lads on the apprenticeship scheme said he heard a clanking and rattling noise coming from the clocktower.'

The elevator.

Markham leaned towards her, his eyes suddenly alight with interest.

'When was this?'

'Some time Monday evening.'

'*Monday!*'

The DI looked at Noakes. 'We saw Mr Belcher on Monday evening.'

'So, he could've been killed later that night, Guv ... even before little Hayley.'

Markham's face darkened. He recalled his last sight of David Belcher's lonely figure at the window of his dingy campaign HQ. And then he saw the man as he had appeared in his dreams – moving like a ghost through the hospital to some phantom operating theatre where he had gestured urgently. '*Look there. Don't you see?*'

I failed to see, the DI reproached himself, and because of that he's dead.

There was something dark and bitter in the remembrance. Even the ending of the dream now appeared charged with significance, the chasm which opened beneath their feet prefiguring Belcher's long descent down the shaft where his body was found.

With an effort, Markham returned to the present.

'He must have seen something,' he said finally. 'Or remembered something and suddenly realized it was significant.'

'But why not come to us, Guv?' Noakes sounded dismayed. 'Why'd he go to the hospital?'

'He must've known it could be dangerous,' Burton put in.

'D'you think it was blackmail, boss? I mean, he didn't seem the type ... unworldly, if you know what I mean.'

'I agree.' Markham's extraordinarily magnetic gaze held his colleagues' attention fast. 'He didn't want money.... I think he worked out who had killed Jonathan Warr and *sympathized* with them.'

'So he wasn't lookin' to turn 'em in?'

'Correct.'

'But what *did* he want then?' Burton was impatient for answers.

'*Information.*'

Calmly and methodically, Markham shared the fruits of his and Noakes's research. Burton listened attentively.

'My God,' she breathed when the DI was finished. 'Maybe that's why this place gives me the creeps.'

Markham looked at her in surprise. Kate Burton rarely said anything so subjective.

Embarrassed, but gratified by his response, she continued, 'Even with all the fancy technology and mod cons, it feels like it might as well be on another continent ... or even on another planet ... as though anything could happen to people if they end up in here....'

'That's zackly 'ow I feel!' exclaimed Noakes.

Despite himself, Markham's lips twitched.

'Well, there you go, kindred spirits the pair of you.'

Seeing that neither looked thrilled at this designation, the DI returned to his analysis.

'David Belcher clearly suspected that some kind of abuse had gone on at the Newman, though it's unlikely he had euthanasia in mind.'

'So you think he wanted someone on the inside to help him figure it out.'

'That's right, Kate. An exposé would have lifted the lid on the Newman as well as giving him more leverage where Mikey was concerned.'

'He took a big risk.'

'I don't think he realized the danger.' The DI's face was downcast. 'His crusading zeal blinded him to everything else.'

'Poor silly lad prob'ly thought he'd end up on *Panorama*.' Noakes bit his lip. 'Why the fuck didn't he come to us instead?'

'He saw us as the "establishment", Noakes. Didn't feel able to trust us. And, frankly, can you blame him? Remember, Mikey had told him one of our lot was involved.'

'Oh God, *Mikey*.'

'Too late to go to intensive care now, Noakes.'

'Yeah, they probably dish out the meds and tuck 'em up the earliest they c'n get away with.'

'We'll break the news tomorrow.'

Burton snapped her pocketbook shut, looking more like a school prefect than ever.

'What's the plan for tomorrow, sir?'

'Briefing at 7 a.m. I'll look at anything else from Doyle then.' Then, ruefully, 'Doctor Warr's funeral is tomorrow afternoon, so best bib and tucker for that. All of us on parade, no exceptions.'

'Blimey, that's quick, Guv. How come?'

'By special request. The family and the Health Trust want it done and dusted quickly and quietly … no fanfare … buried on an inside page of the *Gazette* rather than front page news, if you get my drift.'

They did.

'And with the body being skeletonized, it was simply a question of taking specimens.'

Organs in jars, as Doctor 'Dimples' Davidson had put it.

Burton swallowed a yawn. 'I'll stay and see the SOCOs off, sir.'

'Me an' all.'

Markham blinked. The *entente cordiale* appeared to be putting out some delicate shoots. Well, far be it from him to look a gift horse in the mouth.

'Excellent,' he said before adding with mock severity, 'but no need to write up a report. That can wait till tomorrow morning.'

'Wouldn't think of it, boss.' In Noakes's case, he had no doubt that was the literal truth.

Thursday afternoon.

Jonathan Warr's funeral in the crematorium chapel at Bromgrove North Municipal Cemetery was quite as grim as Markham had anticipated.

Walking up the gravel path which bordered the garden of remembrance, the DI was surprised to see Muriel Noakes bearing down on him, resplendent in an extraordinary black toque reminiscent of defunct royalty. She had Noakes in custody, which doubtless explained why he looked almost passable, though the way he was wriggling – like a small boy who needed the loo – suggested his dark suit was much too tight.

Markham realized he was staring. Hastily, he rearranged his features into an expression of bland good will.

'Good afternoon, Gilbert.'

God, those dreadful arch tones. And she was the only person who ever called him Gilbert.

'Hello, Muriel. This is an unexpected pleasure.'

'Well, one tries to support the local community.'

One. Queen Mother setting.

Markham carefully avoided looking at Noakes.

'Olivia not with you?' She made it sound like a dereliction of duty. But then, he was well aware that Muriel didn't regard his girlfriend as "officer class", while Noakes's dumb crush only increased her jealous resentment.

And yet, Markham knew that Noakes was devoted to his pushy social-climbing wife and fiercely defensive, as though he saw something in her that others – less observant – missed. Champion ballroom performers, on the dance floor the apparently ill-assorted couple moved in perfect harmony.

He reminded himself not to judge by appearances. What do we ever really know about what goes on in other people's lives, he wondered.

Somehow, he needed to find time to catch up with Olivia. Bridge the distance that had mysteriously arisen between them. Until now, hers was the thread of Ariadne whose lightest touch brought him back. But now the thread was unravelling. Something threatened the link between them....

As he stood lost in thought (so *alone*, Muriel hissed, not at all *sotto voce*), there was a general drift towards the chapel. Kate Burton and Doyle came up alongside him looking as ill at ease as Noakes with the same air of clothes pinching uncomfortably, in the metaphorical if not literal sense.

'The DCI and Chief Super have already gone in,' Burton whispered.

'Right, we'll slip in near the back,' Markham replied.

The chapel's exterior was quaintly mock gothic, but inside it had all the charm of a downmarket garden centre. Plastic flowers, greenish-yellow uplighting which gave the mourners' faces an anaemic cast, and a terracotta plinth for the coffin. The only religious emblem was a hideous kitsch crucifix dangling from a hook next to the reader's pine lectern. Mustard-yellow curtains framed a proscenium arch with little doors leading to the furnace and chimney beyond. For a wrenching moment, Markham was reminded of the mouse-hole hatch through which David Belcher's body had made its last journey.

Quickly, he looked away and surveyed the congregation. It was noticeably small but, with a cloud hanging over the good doctor's reputation, that was perhaps not surprising. Slimy Sid and Chief Superintendent Rees were there, however, mounting a rear-guard action. Philip Rees must have felt the DI's eyes boring into his back, because he turned around and gave a chilly nod. Sensing an inscrutable falsehood behind the executive veneer, Markham suddenly felt more convinced than ever that Rees and Warr had been partners. The consultant's path had been smoothed. Records deleted and protest stifled. For a price.

On the other side of the aisle, he noticed a small contingent from the hospital. Linda Harelock and Ernie Roberts looked as though they were propping each other up. Anna Sladen, graceful in a tailored black dress and blazer, kept glancing at them in concern. Doctor Lopez and Sister Appleton wore expressions of professional sympathy but that was only to be expected. Claire Holder's appearance, on the other hand, came as a shock. Looking as though she had aged twenty years, like Muriel Noakes she was wearing some over-the-top millinery – a veiled riding hat more appropriate to costume drama than a low-key funeral. From her glassy-eyed stare, Markham suspected tranquilizers or drink.

The service was mercifully restrained and 'undenominational', the elderly celebrant dispensing with a eulogy. A knocked-about looking blonde gave the reading, her voice flat, almost bored.

"'Though I speak with the tongues of men and of angels, and have not charity, I am become as sounding brass, or a tinkling cymbal.'"

This was presumably Warr's widow, to whom Superintendent Bretherton had broken the news of her husband's demise. According to rumour, she appeared less than grief-stricken.

Charity, thought Markham. My God. Rage flushed through his entire body as he remembered Jonathan Warr's wretched end, and he realized he was shaking. Unobtrusively, he crammed his hands into the pockets of his pin striped suit.

A canned version of 'Jerusalem' brought the proceedings to an end, what remained of Doctor Jonathan Warr creeping inch by inch on its conveyor belt towards the little doors. Then the coffin was gone and they could go.

The wooded grounds of the crematorium were like something out of *Hansel and Gretel*, Markham thought as they emerged into the small leafy park. Fairy tale-ish and surreal. He was glad the chimney was obscured by tall pines.

It felt obligatory to gather round the wreaths. Amongst some ostentatiously flamboyant wreaths, the DI was touched to see a small bouquet of red roses and dianthus. *From the befrienders.* Behind it nestled a simple nosegay of violets with a card that read *Ernie and all the Porters.*

People began to disperse. Markham saw Anna Sladen shepherding Linda and Ernie away. Doctor Lopez walked with Sister Appleton and Claire Holder. A gaggle of hospital staff followed.

Markham decided he couldn't face an encounter with Slimy Sid or the Chief Super. Good. Muriel Noakes had buttonholed them while her husband and his colleagues stood awkwardly on the side lines.

'We're out of here,' he told his officers briskly. 'And before you ask, Noakes, no, there isn't a wake. Or at least not one at which our presence is requested.'

The DS was clearly disappointed by the lack of an opportunity to demonstrate his fabled proficiency at hoovering up vol au vents and canapés.

'Best get out of the monkey suits then,' he muttered sulkily, glowering at the DCI as though he held him personally responsible. 'I bet they're going to the eats.' Noakes was nothing if not a good hater.

'You and I are going on a little trip,' Markham said to the disgruntled DS. Turning to Burton and Doyle, he instructed, 'Chase up the PM on David Belcher. Then re-interview every member of staff and check the whereabouts of all patients from Monday evening.' Noting Doyle's air of discouragement, he rallied the young detective. 'Kate will brief you on what Noakes and I have turned up so far. We are getting closer, but there's a conspiracy of silence here.' Lowering his voice, he added, 'One which goes right to the top. So be discreet.'

'What about the archive records?' Burton asked.

'Keep digging. I want as much as you can find on those patients and their surgery.'

She felt a sharp flare of resentment. Why did the DI keep her at arm's length? Why did Noakes always get the plum assignments? Why was she always palmed off with the desk jobs when what she craved was to be out in the field?

Aware of the DI looking at her, she summoned an expression of geisha-like submission, but inside the hard bitter feeling was getting pretty bad. Unfair, unfair, she raged silently.

'Everything all right, Kate?' Markham's keen gaze raked her face. It would be too humiliating if he guessed her thoughts.

'Absolutely, boss.'

One day she'd be able to show him, she thought. One day soon.... The DCI and Chief Super were looking restive.

'Let's travel,' he said.

Footsteps crunched on the gravel.

Gradually, peace returned to the crematorium grounds. Only the tall pines twisted and writhed as if there were secrets they would tell if they could.

10

A Mystery

CONVERSATION ON THE LONG drive to Seacrest was desultory, but Markham and Noakes were perfectly comfortable together. 'Like a pair of old slippers,' as Olivia was wont to put it.

Before attending Jonathan Warr's funeral, they had visited the intensive care ward at the Newman to break the news of his brother's death to Mikey Belcher. The DI had suggested that DC Doyle accompany them, feeling that the experience would prove beneficial to the young officer.

'An' a fat lot of use he turned out to be,' groused the DS. 'Kept looking round like he couldn't wait to be out of it.'

'I think you're being a little hard on him,' Markham demurred. 'Dealing with bereaved relatives is difficult at the best of times.' There was silence while both men recalled their traumatic visit to Hayley Macdonald's parents on Tuesday after the discovery of her body, her mother going into complete nervous shock at their announcement so that a doctor had to be called to administer a strong sedative. 'And let's face it, the locked ward of a special hospital isn't your average set-up.'

'He was a right snowflake.' Noakes was having none of it.

'Goggling at that poor lad like he had three heads.'

'Pot, kettle, black,' Markham responded with some asperity. 'I seem to recall you were pretty spooked yourself by the Newman to start with.'

'Yeah, but that Mikey, he's all right.' The DS spoke gruffly. 'Got more sense than the medicos, if you ask me.'

Markham suppressed a smile. 'Maybe you and Mikey clicked because you're both Yorkshiremen. "God's own country" and all that.'

'Got our heads screwed on the right way, you mean.'

'Hmmm.'

Something was troubling Noakes. 'When we told him about David, it was almost like he'd been expecting it. Like it were fate or summat.'

It was true. Mikey Belcher had said nothing when the DI told him of the two previous murders, and his response to the news of his brother's death was simply, 'Dave won't be coming then.' Sister Appleton had borne down on them at that point, but Noakes had interposed himself between nurse and patient before telling her to 'Bugger off!'

'Mikey's on pretty strong meds, remember.' Markham was gentle. 'That's why his response seemed flat.'

'Poor bastard, having to cope with the gruesome twosome….'

Markham sighed. 'You weren't exactly diplomatic, Sergeant.'

'Well, I jus' don't *like* 'em, Guv.' The DS cherished his prejudices. 'Lopez is all teeth. Like Tony Blair. An' that nurse is a right cold piece. The way she looked at Mikey, her face would've curdled milk.'

'Well, at least Anna Sladen's dropping by to spend time with him this afternoon, that's some comfort.'

'You like that one.' A statement, not a question.

Markham became aware the DS was watching him

appraisingly, almost wistfully, as though apprehensive of clouds on the horizon.

That was the trouble with Noakes. The grizzled copper was just like a child when it came to concealing his emotions – at least where Olivia was concerned. He seemed to have settled into the role of faithful servitor, as though into the foundations of a building. And Markham's faith in his ever budging from that position was not much greater than if he actually *had* been a building.

For all his exasperation, the DI was touched. He and Olivia each knew that the other liked Noakes, and that he loved them both. It was the strangest of eternal triangles.

And now, with that acuity of a jealous lover, Noakes had sensed the presence of a cloud, though it was as yet no bigger than a man's hand.

'Ms Sladen struck me as a caring and sensitive professional,' Markham said carefully.

'Oh aye.' Noakes was cool. As much as to admit there might be other goddesses but he preferred to worship at his own exclusive shrine.

A change of subject was called for.

'I've told Kate and Doyle to re-interview Claire Holder and go in hard this time.'

The tactic was successful.

'D'you think she's hiding summat, Guv? I mean, the woman lost it big time up there on the roof.'

'Oh, she knows something all right.' Markham's voice hardened. 'And if it turns out that she withheld information that could have stopped a killing spree, then I'll nail her to the wall.'

There was a long silence.

'That service for Warr fair turned my guts.' Noakes was angry. 'Pillar of the community an' all that, when he was really a murdering bastard 'isself.'

'Yes, it was horrible.' The DI spoke with feeling.

'An' the DCI an' Chief Super there an' all.' The DS choked. 'When the Chief Super's likely in it up to his neck.... I mean, *Magnum*, for fuck's sake, it's gotta be him.'

'We've only got circumstantial evidence on Rees. The CPS would laugh us out of court. Mikey would never stand up to cross-examination ... we couldn't put him through it.'

'It's gotta be Rees,' Noakes said obstinately. 'Doyle said a couple of the porters were gassing about him practically having the run of the place. Like Jimmy Savile in Broadmoor, they said. Ernie Roberts shut them up pronto.' A reluctant chuckle. 'Doyle said the old boy looked proper shocked by the way they were carrying on.'

'All circumstantial, Sergeant.'

'Yeah, I know.' The DS thumped the dashboard by way of giving relief to his feelings.

'And you can stop vandalizing my car,' Markham added mildly.

'How are we going to get him, then?'

'Well, I want a search warrant for Ted Cartwright's office. But—'

'Sidney'd have your balls on a plate.'

'In a word, yes.'

'So we're stuffed.'

'I think there may be a way round it.'

'Yeah?'

'Kate has a contact over at the council.'

'Like a *snout*?'

'Frankly, I'm not enquiring too closely, Sergeant. This is all on the QT.'

'What's the plan then? Breaking and entering?' Noakes's

tone was derisive. 'You're not telling me Little Miss Muffet's up to that kind of caper!'

'I prefer to think of it as a discreet recce … into Cartwright's office using a pass key followed by a quick look at his files.'

'What if Cartwright comes back?'

'He won't. He at the university most of Friday delivering – God, the irony of it! – a course on Ethics to Bromgrove's budding legal eagles.'

'What if he's moved the incriminating stuff out of his office?'

'Something tells me he hasn't.' Markham frowned at the road ahead. 'Cartwright's arrogant, you see. Just like Warr.' He shrugged. 'If I'm wrong, it's back to the drawing board, but if not … well, we could hit pay dirt.'

'Cartwright's computer?'

'Shouldn't be a problem, so Kate assures me.'

Noakes was clearly torn between his traditional resentment of the department clever clogs and an equally deep-rooted desire to cock a snook at the local hegemony.

'That slimy shit's been riding for a fall,' he grunted.

From which Markham deduced that Noakes's subversive instincts had come out on top.

It was now dark.

'We won't see much of Sea … whatever it's called…'

'Seacrest. That's why I told you to pack a bag, Sergeant,' Markham said patiently. 'I've booked us into a B&B in Holkham for tonight.' And we can't get there soon enough, he thought, registering the dull ache in his lower back. 'It'll do us good to be away from the Newman for a bit. Breathe some sea air … take stock.'

He felt guilty about not giving Kate Burton a turn, but knew she was better deployed back at base keeping the pressure on Holder and the rest, her terrier-like instincts focused on running clues to ground. She could also be relied on to send up the requisite smoke signals in the event that DCI Sidney became importunate. Noakes was useless when it came to finessing their superiors, whereas Burton's quick thinking was invaluable in such situations.

Deep down, Markham knew that Kate was hurt by his reserve and apparent preference for Noakes. But he also knew that he wasn't ready to allow her too close – that he was afraid to give too much away. One day, he told himself, but not just yet...

His spirits drooping, he asked himself why he had decided to visit Seacrest, telephone calls having elicited the information that there were currently only a skeleton staff on site.

'What're you expecting to find, Guv?'

It was almost uncanny the way the DS knew what his boss was thinking.

'That's just it, Noakesy,' Markham said lamely, 'I've no idea. Somehow, I'm hoping this place will *speak* to me ... that I'll pick up the vibrations from those poor lost souls who were hidden away....'

'Out of sight, out of mind,' Noakes concluded for him.

'Exactly.' There was an overwhelming sense of relief that the DS understood. 'I can't get it out of my head ... keep imagining some man or woman, regressed into an infant-like state, maybe mumbling a few words, sitting for hours staring at the walls.... While the world outside pretended that nothing had ever happened and they no longer existed. No visits. Nothing.'

'Nasty,' Noakes agreed, not in the least fazed by the reference to psychic emanations, as though it was eminently reasonable that Markham should want to hook up with the ghosts of folk who had endured botched lobotomies and God knows what else.

'Have they got Sky at this B&B, boss? Bromgrove Wanderers are playing away, see, an' I've got a score on our lads.'

'I imagine so ... in any event, we can always watch it in the bar.'

'An' another thing.'

'Your wish is my command, Sergeant.'

'Any chance of going round by Sandringham on the way back?'

'I'm not scaling the fence to spy on royalty.'

'Nah, Guv ... it's just ... I c'n tell the missus ... she loves the Queen.'

Markham felt a great wave of affection for his big awkward subordinate. He was such a very *human* human being. Had it been Kate Burton with him, interminable shop talk would have been the order of the day. And he really didn't care to imagine her likely reaction to psychic communings down by the beach....

'Too much sky,' Noakes pronounced on Friday morning as they took in the landscape surrounding Seacrest.

The DI understood what he meant. Paradoxically, there was something oppressive about the sweeping breadth of the horizon, which reduced the countryside to a huge circular enclosure: a coliseum where human beings crawled like ants beneath the gaze of an inscrutable and hostile deity. The grass-fringed sandhills, bounded by a great black sheet of water stretching out to meet the sky, were desolate enough to fill him with profound depression. Even in the day's vigorous prime, there was a sense of solitude and sadness. As though the spongy ground sought to draw travellers down, down into its opaque depths.

Hastily, Markham roused himself. 'Those are the chalets, over there. The same as in the photograph.'

'Right enough,' Noakes concurred unenthusiastically. 'But ain't there some kind of reception place ... y'know, somewhere to ... book in or what have you?'

'It must be that building across to the left. The log cabin affair just in front of that grove of trees.'

'Not much to write home about.' The DS was unimpressed. 'Jus' like a camping site.'

But the isolation was perfect, Markham thought, a chill stealing over his heart....

The current wardens of Seacrest, Bob and Mary Seacombe, turned out to be a couple of retirees and passionate ornithologists to boot. Once they'd established their visitors' grievous ignorance of bittern and bullfinches, the supply of small talk was pretty much exhausted.

'We're fairly new,' Mrs Seacombe said in warm comfortable tones which were curiously at odds with her surroundings. 'Been here around a year and a half now.'

'That's right.' Bob Seacombe was a homely, weathered-looking man whose deeply lined and bronzed face and thick mane of iron-grey hair falling almost to his shoulders stamped him as a former sea captain. His diction too had something quaintly nautical about it. 'It's a snug berth for us here.... Only light watchkeeping seeing as there ain't much call for respite holidays lately.... The last time anyone came was just before we started.'

'No money for extras these days.' His wife nodded sagely. 'Seems a shame.'

Cordial but apparently incurious, the pair accepted at face value Markham's vague reference to an ongoing investigation and promptly handed over keys to the cottages.

'They're numbered one to eight, as you can see. If you walk along the path about a hundred yards from the last one, you'll find the loos and shower block. Just beyond that there's the ECT suite.'

'The *what?*'

'Careful, Mother.' Bob cautioned his wife with a rueful chuckle. 'Remember, it's not called that anymore.'

Mrs Seacombe appeared flustered. 'Oh yes, silly of me. I just call it that because apparently they did electroshock therapy in there long ago and the name stuck.'

'It's all non-invasive treatments now, isn't it?' her husband said cheerfully. 'Ceramics and basket-weaving, that kind of thing.'

'*Basket-weaving!*' Noakes burst out when they were well out of earshot. '*An' freakin' ceramics!* What planet are those two on?!'

'They're just very unworldly, Sergeant, and conveniently uninterested in pretty much everything outside bird-watching.'

'Just as well you turned down tea, Guv. Good call. They'd be jabbering on about mallards and sodding geese till fuck knows when. Prob'ly try to get us signed up into the bargain.'

'I thought you'd approve,' Markham said gravely.

'Did you clock what Captain Nemo said about visits dropping off?'

'Just before Doctor Warr went missing....'

'The same time them investigations into patient abuse were getting started.'

'Yes.' Markham spoke in a low halting voice, as though fearful the rustling grasses might catch his words. 'It was all too close for comfort. So ... business was suspended.'

Inside the huts, Markham felt nothing at all. No vibrations. Nothing.

What had he expected, he asked himself, feeling foolish. They were just dusty empty spaces, with no trace in their modest wooden bedsteads and little galley kitchens of any former occupants.

It was outside, on the path that wound round the cottages, that Markham had an extra sensory awareness of evil. He knew he felt it in that narrow weed-choked space. The air was icy, the pine trees crippled and stunted. Suddenly, he wanted very much to be away from Seacrest and all its works.

'Guv?' Noakes had sensed his discomfort.

'Let's have a quick look at that ECT block she mentioned and then we're off.' He looked at the DS apologetically. 'There's nothing for us here.'

As with the chalets, the two cabins which comprised the treatment suite were bare save for two long benches running the length of each room. While Noakes prowled the perimeter, testing the barred windows, Markham closed his eyes and briefly imagined a faceless patient lying on an operating table, head placed on a sandbag, waiting for a spatula to destroy the white matter of the brain....

What happened at Seacrest? Did anyone try to escape? Did patients die here, or were they carried along that overgrown path to somewhere even more remote, even more secluded ... beyond the reach of all human aid?

'Zilch, Guv. No hypodermics or scalpels. Someone gave this place a good clear out.'

Barely repressing a shudder, Markham began to lead the way in silence back across the dunes.

'Hold on a sec, Guv.'

'What?'

'Well, aren't we going to check out that path round the back?'

'Which path?'

'There's a little tow path or summat. I saw it from the back window. Dontcha want to see where it goes?'

'Lead on, Sergeant,' Markham said, resigned to further exploration.

The two men walked round to the back of the treatment block where a dirt track led to a broken gate. Beyond this was a scrubby field with roughly cropped grass and a couple of stunted yews.

Passing through the gate, as they advanced into the field they came across sunken gravestones and lopsided blackened crosses choked by nettles, but there was no church or any other building to be seen. A curlew wheeled overhead, keening mournfully, otherwise nothing stirred.

Markham scanned the derelict scene. 'There must have been a church at some time.'

'Wouldn't fancy pushing up the daisies in here,' Noakes said. 'It's proper depressing.'

The DI felt a prickling between his shoulder blades.

Slowly, he turned 360 degrees.

'What's that?' he said at last.

'Where?'

'Over there by the wall.'

Markham led the way to some delapidated, moss-encrusted burial vaults crudely assembled from local bricks and boulders. There were no plaques or markers. Nothing to identify the sleepers in their tumbledown resting place.

'Jus' some crumbly old tombs,' Noakes sniffed. 'Look at all them weeds. You'd think someone could make a bit of an effort ... show some respect, like.'

Markham bent down to take a closer look. 'I think someone may have had a go at tidying up ... there's some fresh grouting—'

'Hey there! Yoo-hoo!'

Yoo-hoo. Noakes sniggered as the Seacombes came plunging

across the field towards them, Mary Seacombe's untidy grey bun coming loose from its moorings in her hurry to waylay them.

'Hello there.' Markham shot the DS a repressive look. 'Quaint little graveyard this. Hope you didn't mind us taking a quick look.'

A shadow passed across Bob Seacombe's bluff weathered face, so fleeting that it was barely discernible except to Markham who watched the couple closely.

'Not at all, Inspector. It's just that the hospital asked us to keep this field out of bounds to visitors ... with it being consecrated ground, you see.' The man twisted his striped neckerchief awkwardly. 'I should've put up a notice or something, but hardly anyone ever comes.'

Too busy watching bloody blue tits, thought Noakes, allowing himself an inner eye roll.

'No worries, Mr Seacombe.' Markham was very smooth. 'High time for us to be making tracks.' On the way back to the reception area, he kept up a stream of light inconsequential chat.

'Would you like to sign the visitors' book?' sang out Mrs Seacombe. 'It's a bit of an event for us what with not seeing anyone from one month to the next ... if you don't count Coastal Care ...' Observing Noakes's refractory expression, her voice trailed away. 'Or maybe you can't ... I mean, if it's confidential ...'

The DI came to her rescue. '*Delighted*, Mrs Seacombe,' he said expansively. He signed with a flourish before flipping through the pages of the morocco-bound book and running his eyes down the blotted columns with every appearance of interest, though his mind was now far away from Seacrest and back at the Newman. Ever the gentleman, no-one save the closest observer could have detected that Markham now begrudged every minute spent lingering at the front desk.

When they were safely back in the car, he turned to the DS. 'Well, I was beginning to feel my crystal ball moment was a complete waste of time, but the Seacombes' reaction when we were looking at that burial site tells me we're onto something.'

'Yeah, reckon there's something we weren't supposed to see.'

'Those vaults had been tampered with at some point.' Markham's face was grim. 'I want to know who and why.' Then he smiled at his companion. 'We'll be coming back to the seaside before this investigation is very much older, Noakes, once we've got all our ducks in a row.'

'An' I'm twenty squids up after last night, Guv,' the DS carolled. 'Seeing as I'm flush,' the DS added with ferrety glee, 'I'll spring for the fish and chips.'

'So it wasn't a total dead loss in the end, Liv.'

Late afternoon, but the lights were on in the living room of their flat as Markham concluded his account.

Olivia smiled. 'Sounds as if George had a good time.'

Noakes had declined the invitation to come in, shifting from one foot to another and smiling goofily as she accused him of playing hooky and leading her boyfriend astray. Eventually, the DS declared, 'Muriel does hot pot Fridays, so I'd best be going.' Patting his jacket pocket with its precious cargo of postcards showing Sandringham through the seasons, he plodded off with one yearning backwards glance.

'I suspect Noakesy's childhood wasn't exactly *Swallows and Amazons*, so after the Seacrest debacle we took a stroll along Holkham Bay.' He rolled his eyes. 'It was all I could do to stop him going for a paddle.'

Olivia shot him a shrewd glance as he sank into his

favourite armchair. Passing him a black coffee, she asked, 'Would you like a shot of something in that?'

'Better not.' He sighed. 'I need to make tracks soon and get back to the Newman. See what Kate Burton's got for me.'

'Poor Kate, stuck at base.' Olivia made a mock pout. 'You'll really have to give her an away day too, you know, otherwise there'll be complaints that George gets all the jollies.'

'Oh, I guarantee she'll be sunk with pure bliss in the *Diagnostic and Statistical Manual of Mental Disorders.*' He laughed mirthlessly. 'Boning up even as we speak.' He shifted restlessly. 'I can't help feeling that there was something right under my nose at Seacrest and I missed it ... something I should have spotted but didn't ... something that slipped away from me.'

'You're tired,' Olivia said matter-of-factly. 'Nothing that a few bouts at Dirty Dickerson's won't sort.'

'It's Doggie, not Dirty, though come to think of it *your* nickname's a better fit.'

'What was Seacrest like, Gil?' With proud sensitivity, she added, 'You know I don't pry, but it might help to talk.'

'Oh, my love.' There was tenderness in Markham's voice. 'That's just it ... I'd built the place up in my mind, but in the end, it was just a collection of pathetic huts like a downmarket caravan site.'

'Something about it got to you, though.'

'Well, there was this path that wound along by the huts. I just had the strongest sensation of *dread* ... a sort of unreasoning terror as if something really evil was waiting there....'

'A troll under the bridge.' Olivia stroked his arm. 'Like in the fairy story *The Three Billy Goats Gruff.*'

Her light-hearted comment punctured the tension.

'Well, the setting was Brothers Grimm, no doubt about that.'

Markham regarded her indulgently. 'Wild and lonesome. But there weren't any trolls about, just two elderly ornithologists.' He told her about the Seacombes. 'Noakes was terrified they were going to thrust a pair of binoculars at him. You should have seen his face when they started talking about their bird hide ... thought he was going to be dragooned up the sand dunes for a spot of twitching. He couldn't get out of there fast enough. It was much better down on Holkham Bay.'

Olivia chuckled. Then a thought struck her. 'So, they didn't know anything about patients coming to Seacrest for respite care or self-catering breaks?'

'It petered out before their time, apparently. They assumed it was down to local authority cost-cutting.'

'What about the caretakers who were there before them? I mean, there must've been other staff who could tell you something.'

'I'll be putting Doyle onto that, but I'm not optimistic.' Markham frowned. 'Anonymous agency staff, difficult to trace ... just melted away from the sound of it.'

'Or paid to disappear.'

'Very probable.' He sighed. 'The Seacombes were afraid of something ... that sinister little graveyard for one thing.... We've got to go back there.... Slimy Sid can go screw himself.'

There was a pause before Olivia spoke again. The subject took Markham by surprise.

'I've started attending the Newman for some regression therapy, Gil.'

Another pause.

'Actually, I was there today.'

I don't like that place, he wanted to scream. I don't want you there. Especially not now.

But his girlfriend's face had that closed look it

sometimes wore, and he knew better than to probe her oyster-like impenetrability.

He felt a wave of burning resentment. Why could she not trust him as he trusted her?

'Perhaps I'll see you around the hospital,' was all he said, careful to keep the edge from his voice.

The interlude of affectionate complicity was over. With a queer little ache in his heart, Markham rose to his feet. 'Duty calls,' he said simply.

11

Out of Joint

THE NEWMAN'S ANTISEPTIC CLINICISM made Markham's eyes ache.
Times and seasons seemed to have no meaning in the hospital,
its gleaming white corridors and strip lighting turning night
into an everlasting day. He felt a sharp sense of dislocation
as he made his way towards the incident room, the reunion
with Olivia having heightened his feeling that the world was
somehow unhappily out of joint.

The DI paused outside the door, smoothing his features into
an expression of imperturbable gravitas, as befitted the SIO on
an increasingly nightmarish murder case.

He found Noakes and Doyle animatedly reviewing the
recent performance of Bromgrove Wanderers, observed by
Kate Burton with a distinctly glazed look in her eyes which
suggested she'd had a bellyful. At Markham's entrance, she
brightened up, practically clicking her heels, so relieved was
she to see him.

'Evening, team.'

Noakes broke off from an engrossing debate about whether
Bromgrove's skipper deserved to be sent off for diving, and

eyed his boss with the squinty-eyed narrowness Markham had learned to dread. His assumed sang-froid might deceive Burton and Doyle, but George Noakes was another matter.

Summat's up with the guvnor, the DS thought to himself. Summat to do with *Olivia* (lingering over her name as a miser his gold). The day suddenly seemed very dark to Noakes though, in the rapture of post-match analysis, it had been very bright the minute before. Even the doughnut snagged from the hospital canteen had lost its allure.

'You okay, Guv?' That was as far as he dared go in front of the others.

The DI forced a smile. 'Just knackered, Sergeant. Like all of you.'

He could tell Noakes wasn't deceived. That mulish look suggested his wingman would return to the charge before the day was very much older. In the meantime, Markham wanted an update.

The DI turned to Burton. 'What news of the PM on David Belcher?'

'Knocked unconscious then strangled, sir.'

At least the poor devil was dead and past his pain before being tipped into the ventilation shaft. There would be some small comfort for Mikey in that.

'How did it go with your contact at the council, Kate? Any problems with access to Ted Cartwright's office?'

'Worked like a dream, sir.' The mischievous grin made Burton look like a schoolgirl who'd "got one over" on the grown ups. 'No-one batted an eyelid. He just did his internet bot number – spouted some gobbledygook at Cartwright's airhead secretary, who was more interested in painting her nails and catching up on office gossip than checking what the geek from IT got up to.' The DS gestured to a folder bulging with papers and printouts. 'This arrived a little while ago.'

'Anything interesting?' Markham asked eagerly.

'Well, I haven't gone through it all yet, sir. But Cartwright was in regular contact with Doctor Warr and the Chief Super all right ... outside official business, from the look of it.' She frowned. 'Parts of the correspondence look like they may be in some sort of code.'

'*Code*?' Noakes guffawed. 'We're talking about Ted Cartwright here, y'know. Not Double O Seven, luv.'

Doyle gave an appreciative snigger.

'Ignore them, Kate.' At the DI's boot-faced expression, further witticisms expired on Noakes's lips.

Markham was thoughtful. 'Code,' he repeated. 'Can you ask your friend to take a look for us?' Burton nodded vigorously. 'But *absolute discretion*, do you understand?' Even more vigorous assent. 'We're talking about a council solicitor and our Chief Super. If the DCI gets wind of it, we're toast ... directing traffic for the rest of our days.'

'Looks like there's other stuff too, sir.'

'Such as?'

'Well, you know those names Cartwright gave us ... the ones we were checking in the archives?'

'Not much doing, as I recall.'

'That's right, sir. But looks like there were a few cases in the late eighties and early nineties that caused ripples.'

'Ripples?' Markham was intrigued.

'As in folk making a fuss ...'

'Go on.'

'There was this patient with learning disabilities called Rose. Well, she had a sister who turned up at the Newman shouting the odds. Made quite a scene from the sound of it.... Claimed that Rose had been sectioned cos she was going to

shoot her mouth off about secrets ... sexual abuse ... stuff the
family didn't want to get out.'

'Who was the abuser?'

'Rose's father.'

'How come our lot weren't involved?' Noakes was dumb-
founded. 'I mean, we're talking *incest* for fuck's sake.'

'Well, this is where it gets interesting, Sarge.' Burton clearly
enjoyed holding the floor, her cheeks flushed with excitement.
'Rose was diagnosed with schizophrenia – hearing voices, out
of touch with reality, the usual – so the sister got short shrift.'
The DS rumpled her neat pageboy, such unwonted dishevel-
ment a sure sign that this particular case history had got
under her skin. 'It was a respectable family ... well-connected.
Reading between the lines, it sounds as though they managed
to get any police involvement closed down pretty much at the
outset.'

'For a price, one assumes.' Markham's tone was dark with
anger.

'What happened to this Rose, then?' Doyle's good-natured
face was unusually indignant. 'Did they just keep her locked
up? Did she even have schizophrenia in the first place?' He
was falling over his words now. 'You can't just *imprison* people.
There's habeas corpus ... stuff like that.' Clearly the young
DC's part-time law classes were bearing fruit, if this allusion
was anything to go by.

The DS raised her hands palm upwards in a gesture of
defeat.

'Who knows? From the sound of it, Rose went into the
Newman with mild retardation and some emotional issues
but ended up a vegetable.... She had ECTs followed by "psy-
chosurgical intervention" which was deemed to be of "limited
effectiveness".' The grimace which accompanied Burton's air

quotes was ample testimony to her disgust. 'The sister only got to see her once afterwards ... she was devastated because Rose wouldn't look at her ... like she thought she'd been abandoned and left to rot.'

'Christ,' Doyle breathed.

'Oh, it gets worse,' Burton said sadly. 'Rose's mum had a breakdown. Never got over the tragedy, absolutely traumatized. Died six months later.'

'Where did Rose end up?' The DI experienced a sense of acute foreboding.

'She was on the intensive care ward to start with.'

Markham thought of those seriously disturbed human beings and the row of locked cells with their reinforced doors. Involuntarily, his hands clenched.

'They don't keep women patients there for long,' Burton said uncomfortably. 'And there's a designated female-only safe space ...'

'Oh, so that's all right then.' Noakes's sarcastic rejoinder hung in the air.

'Of course it's not all right!' the DS burst out. 'I feel as bad about it as you do!'

'Shut up, Noakes.'

'I only meant ter say—'

'Button it, Sergeant.' It was a tone which brooked no dissent.

Noakes subsided, muttering to himself, 'A right poor do ...'

The DI turned back to Burton. 'It's a wretched story, Kate. I can see it's upset you.'

'What happened in the end?' Doyle asked impatiently.

'I'm guessing once Rose was stabilized it was medium secure care for a while, then she must've been discharged to a step-down unit.'

'Eh?' Noakes was staging a rapid comeback from Markham's

rebuke. 'What's one of those when it's at home?'

'Like a rehabilitation centre ... somewhere to prepare her for life in the community.'

'You said you were "guessing", Kate? How come?'

'Well, sir, the paper trail seems to go cold after she left the Newman.... That or there's gaps in the records.'

'Paperwork conveniently lost, you mean.' The DI's lips were tightly compressed.

'The sister didn't give up ... kept badgering. But Rose had requested there be no contact with family.'

A spark kindled far down in Markham's dark eyes.

'She didn't have capacity.'

Burton shrugged helplessly. 'There was lasting power of attorney. The father and older brothers claimed to be consult-ing Rose's wishes. There were other younger siblings who'd been affected by her violent outbursts in the past ... seems to have been accepted all round that it'd be easier to park her in an institution somewhere.'

Suddenly, as vividly as if the image was imprinted on his retina, Markham pictured a narrow brick vault full of bones. A young woman's bones.

'I don't think Rose ever found her way back home,' he said quietly, before telling Burton and Doyle about the lonely little graveyard at Seacrest.

When he had finished, there was dead silence.

'Are you saying patients like Rose were being *murdered* for convenience, sir?'

'Or, to be put it another way, *euthanized*.' The DI looked steadily at Doyle who was visibly shaken. 'Chronic neglect, starvation and medication "mix ups" would probably do the trick, so no need for more overt measures.'

'They murdered her mum too,' Doyle said passionately.

'Well, she had emphysema,' Burton answered. 'But learning about the botched operation sent her into a depression … it was all done behind her back you see. She nearly ended up in the Newman herself … in the end she just lost the will to live.'

'Do we have a surname for Rose?'

'From what I've seen, it's just initials. RS.' Burton looked discouraged. 'And for all we know, sir, *they* mightn't be genuine.'

'Any names of medical personnel?'

The DS shook her head. 'It's all very secret squirrel, boss. Doctor X and Nurse Y, that kind of thing.'

'Huh,' Noakes spat out venomously. 'We all know it was them two, wasn't it? Kennedy an' Molloy … not forgetting the boy wonder hisself.'

'Boy wonder?' Doyle echoed in bewilderment.

'Keep up, shit-for-brains,' the DS riposted amicably. '*Jonathan Warr*, of course. He'd 've been in his late thirties then, working up to being a consultant like them.' He turned to the DI, 'What d'you think Warr's cut was?'

'This is all conjecture, people.' Markham was tense.

DC Doyle was fidgeting with paperclips, as though revolving something in his mind.

'What is it, Doyle?'

'Ted Cartwright and the Chief Super weren't on the scene till much later, sir – 2010…. So where do they fit into all this?'

'We have to see Doctor Warr's activities in terms of phases.' Reluctant pity for the murdered consultant lanced through him. 'I think there were stretches when he probably managed to fulfil the role of dedicated, caring professional. But then a combination of greed and megalomania somehow came into play, and he was seduced back into ethically dubious magic surgery.'

'With Cartwright and Rees oiling the wheels,' Noakes finished glumly.

'Yes.' To Markham there was now a ghastly inevitably about that unholy troika. 'They served on the same local committees ... mixed with the great and the good ... attended the same case conferences....'

'Had their snouts in the same trough.'

'It seems increasingly likely.' The DI was quietly circumspect. 'Though I should stress we need to be wary of jumping to conclusions. All of this is just hypothesis.' Sombrely, he added, 'It doesn't take us any closer to finding out who killed Hayley Macdonald and David Belcher.'

'Any chance of an exhumation licence for the graveyard at Seacrest, sir?'

'It would take time. Which is something we don't have.'

'An' 'sides, the DCI'd never wear it,' Noakes pointed out. 'What with it pointing the finger at Warr an' his cronies.'

Only too true, thought Markham, wincing at the thought of Slimy Sid's likely reaction if he attempted to revisit the theory of corruption in high places. He could hear it now. 'Have you forgotten that Doctor Warr is the *victim* here, Inspector?' That would be followed by the usual folderol about besmirching the reputations of public servants, and the coda would follow the familiar lines of a warning against his besetting sin – *flair*.

No, far better to keep feeding Sidney the line that they were focusing their attention on psychopaths with a grudge while secretly following the psychosurgery trail.

The problem was that he couldn't stall Sidney forever. Any time now, the DCI's love of PR meant that he would be demanding Markham set up a press conference where he could announce, in statesmanlike fashion, that the police were on the verge of a significant breakthrough.

Only problem being they currently had zilch.

The DI dragged his attention back to the team.

'Kate, you said you'd come across a few cases in Cartwright's files that caused ripples.'

'That's right, sir.' Intelligent brown eyes watched him intently.

'Were they like Rose's?'

'Well, hers stood out, sir, cos of the way the family went smash. The mum dying like that and a couple of the younger kids going off the rails.... But there were one or two other cases where people made complaints.' She screwed up her face in an effort to recall the details. 'There was one woman whose husband cut up rough about Warr using hypnotherapy. He claimed she was never really the same afterwards.... I think she ended up in the Newman again after an attempted suicide. The husband wrote to the CEO of the Health Trust as well as his MP, but no dice.'

'Sounds like the good doctor was untouchable.' The bitterness in Doyle's voice attracted Markham's attention. He noticed that Noakes was covertly scrutinizing him as well. The DS had an avuncular relationship with Doyle, regularly appraising the youngster's amatory prospects and the fortunes of their beloved Bromgrove Wanderers (it was debatable as to which loomed larger) over a pint. The old war horse was bound to know what was up. Once they'd finished here, Markham would winkle it out of him.

'One thing I don't get, boss.'

'What's that, Kate?'

'Why did Cartwright have all this stuff from the eighties and nineties in his files? As Doyle said, he only arrived on the scene much later.'

'A way of making sure Warr stayed in line,' Noakes

suggested. 'If Cartwright knew where the bodies were buried,' his three colleagues flinched, 'then he could put the screws on Warr. No chance of the doc bottling out.'

'Insurance.' The DI's voice rang with conviction. 'He wanted to make sure that nothing from Warr's earlier practice could come back to bite them.'

'And now it has.'

'Yes,' Markham said seriously. 'I imagine Ted Cartwright is one very frightened man.'

'Good.' Noakes's response was unequivocal.

'It's getting late.' The DI spoke briskly, trying to inject some energy into his voice. 'Kate, I need you to check out everything we've got from Cartwright, especially those cases where there were complaints against Doctor Warr. See if you can get a handle on the families. Try Social Services, the Health Trust … Citizens Advice … local MP's Constituency Office … mental health support groups. Someone out there knows something that could lead us to the killer.'

'Speaking of support groups, sir, the befrienders are running a coffee morning here tomorrow.' She flashed a grin at Noakes. 'Lots of home baking, so Linda Harelock tells me.'

'S'pose we oughta show our faces, Guv. Community relations an' all that.'

'Absolutely, Sergeant,' Markham replied. 'I know I can rely on you to consume sufficient quantities of Bakewell tart to disarm the most obdurate critic of Bromgrove CID.'

Noakes wasn't at all sure he liked the guvnor's sarky tone of voice. But he wasn't about to look a gift horse in the mouth. 'My Muriel never misses Mary Berry,' he said loftily. 'Happen she'll drop in. With it being for charity.'

The DI suppressed a groan.

'Doyle, I'll catch up with you first thing tomorrow. See where we're up to with staff and patient movements. Right, you and Kate shoot off. Noakes, a quick word, please.'

When the door had shut behind the other two, he asked bluntly, 'What's the matter with Doyle?' As the other hesitated, he rapped, 'There's no point denying it, Sergeant. It was written all over his face.'

'His older sister Jean's retarded.'

'Learning disabled, Noakes.'

'Whatever.' Noakes was unabashed. 'Epileptic too.'

'I'm sorry to hear that. Presumably that's why he was so uncomfortable visiting Mikey Belcher on the intensive care ward.'

'Nah. He was jus' being a big girl's blouse.' The DS drew himself up with almost Churchillian hauteur. 'I told him there's no room for wusses in our nick.'

There was no danger that the quality of mercy would ever be strained in Bromgrove CID, thought Markham. Aloud he said, 'He seemed pretty upset just now.'

'Yeah, well, I s'pose that story Burton was telling got to him.' Noakes cleared his throat. 'He was always watching out for Jean when they were growing up. Hated it when she got called moron an' stuff like that. Other kids were unkind, y'see. When she got into a state, he could calm her down no matter what.'

'You seem to know quite a lot about her.' Markham never failed to marvel at the way his uncouth, monumentally tactless sergeant somehow had the knack of finding his way to people's hearts.

The DS looked embarrassed. 'Well, the lad's dead fond of Jean. She's in one of them assisted living thingies now, but he takes her out at weekends for treats an' that. She's even been to the footie.' He looked straight at Markham. 'I think he was always afraid summat bad might happen ... that they might lock her up an' throw away the key ... or she'd end up in one of them God awful places that smells of pee where they all sit around staring into space.'

'If Jean had fallen into the clutches of a pair of butchers like Kennedy and Molloy, that might well have been her fate.' Markham shuddered.

'You won't tell the lad I've said owt, will you, Guv?' Noakes asked anxiously. 'Only he wouldn't like to think we'd been talking about it.'

'Mum's the word, Sergeant.' Markham smiled warmly at his subordinate, grateful for his infallible radar. 'In the meantime, let's steer Doyle away from those case histories.'

'Burton's welcome to 'em,' the other grunted. 'Like a freaking ghoul she is. Poring over them creepy books from Warr's office.'

Creepy was the word, Markham silently agreed, thinking about sepia pictures of butter knives slicing through brain tissue and paralyzed patients grimacing at the camera, heads tilted, frozen somewhere near their left shoulder, their fingers gnarled and useless. How terrible for Doyle if that had been the phantom of his imagination. His sister spirited away to become the madwoman in the attic.

'Thanks for telling me, Noakesy,' he said sincerely. 'Keep an eye on Doyle for me, will you.'

'Wilco, Guv.' Noakes was proud to have the boss's confidence.

'Right, see you tomorrow, ready to consume your bodyweight in cakes.'

Watching Noakes in action the following morning, winning hearts and minds as he wolfed down chocolate cake and brownies, Markham realized his parting injunction the night before was destined to be followed to the letter.

'It's a pleasure to bake for a man who appreciates home cooking like you do, Sergeant.' Linda Harelock beamed her approval, while her helpers twittered admiringly on the sidelines.

Muriel Noakes, fussily overdressed as always, found time in between patronizing the hospital volunteers to tell Markham in a stage whisper that he was looking 'terribly *thin* and *run down*', before enquiring with misplaced flirtatiousness, 'Whatever is Olivia *doing* to you, Gilbert?' Tempted to reply that a diet of rampant sex was responsible, the sight of Noakes hovering in the background like a faithful St. Bernard checked any tendency to flippancy. Instead, the DI proffered some conventional platitudes which appeared to satisfy Mrs Noakes, for she patted her stiffly lacquered hair with an air of complacent satisfaction before moving on to her next victim, Councillor Edwards, a timid little man who visibly quailed as she bore down on him like a ship in full sail.

Looking around the small café, Markham saw Anna Sladen looking distinctly ill at ease, cornered by Philip Rees of all people. Now, why had the Chief Super bothered to turn up, he asked himself.

The DI allowed himself the pleasure of a few moments' contemplation of Anna's cool blonde beauty, wondering idly what her hair would be like unbound. Danae in her cloud.

Then he caught Noakes's beady eye from across the room and blushed as though he had been caught out in some infidelity. *Damn the man.* What did he think he was? Markham's *chaperone*?

The psychologist's eyes invited him to come and rescue her. Ignoring Noakes, he walked over. Rees was clearly displeased at the interruption.

'Inspector,' he said curtly before turning on his heel and walking across to Claire Holder who stood in a huddle with Doctor Lopez, Sister Appleton and other hospital staff.

The managing director looked less than her glamorous self, wearing a boxy black suit that drained all the colour from her already ravaged face. The rest darted furtive glances at Markham, as though avid to discern if *they* were the subject of conversation.

'You don't relish these occasions, Ms Sladen,' he observed.

'Am I that obvious?' She gave a strained laugh. Close up, he could see dark shadows under the startlingly blue eyes. 'I can't recall who it was talked about every man being surrounded by a neighbourhood of voluntary spies, but they must surely have had the Newman in mind!'

Markham's lips quirked in amusement.

And then he noticed something.

Chief Superintendent Philip Rees was no longer in the café.

'Excuse me, Ms Sladen,' he murmured.

Swiftly, he moved along corridors, glancing into bays, court-yards and day rooms.

There was no-one about save for Ernie Roberts trundling his squeaky-wheeled trolley. Typically selfless, thought Markham. Holding the fort while the rest of them stuffed their faces.

As though by instinct, he directed his steps towards Jonathan Warr's office.

The door was ajar, and through the half-open gap, Markham saw the unmistakable figure of Philip Rees standing next to the consultant's filing cabinet. Stealth was written all over him.

Quietly, hardly daring to breathe, Markham retreated down the corridor.

But there was another watcher, mindful that the time was close at hand.

For we must all appear before the judgment seat to answer for the things done in the body, be they good or bad.

12

Out of the Depths

TURNING A CORNER INTO one of the Newman's endless bays, the DI slumped against the wall collecting his thoughts.

What was the Chief Super doing in Jonathan Warr's office? Who had unlocked it for him? What was Rees looking for?

Wearily, he shut his eyes.

A prickling apprehension recalled Markham to himself. Despite the silence, he felt sure that someone was watching him.

He moved out of the bay to stand in the corridor, scrutinizing its linoleumed depths with a searching mistrust before looking down to the swing doors at the far end.

Suddenly, he saw a face distorted with rage flattened against the glass pane of the left-hand door, cyanosed features contorted in a Munch-like silent scream.

For a minute, Markham stood paralyzed, as though the sight had cast a spell on him, then he moved swiftly down the corridor towards the doors.

There was no-one there, though; like a floater in his eye, he felt that dark silhouette lingering in the cool sanitized hospital air.

Maybe he'd just imagined the apparition, though the sense of scorching hatred had been so strong he had felt as though it might strip the flesh from his bones.

Hell is empty. And all the devils are here.

Christ, this glassed-in greenhouse unnerved him, he thought, moodily gazing out into one of the interconnecting courtyards where colourless sunlight slanted onto concrete under a pumice-grey sky.

The DI felt he couldn't take more forced civility at the coffee morning, so he headed for the incident room. He'd check in with Burton and Doyle before returning to collect Noakes who was no doubt still carrying the flag for CID – right down to the very last crumb.

Burton had a queer, intent look on her face when the DI caught up with her. Bent over what looked like one of the books from Jonathan Warr's extensive library, she appeared both fascinated and repelled.

'Doctor Warr was majorly interested in far-out stuff like genetic engineering and selective breeding, sir.' She gestured to some other volumes at her elbow. 'Eugenics too.'

'Ah. Survival of the fittest.'

'It's totally warped, boss.' Her voice was appalled. 'I mean all this about humanity being made up of different "races" and the "superior" ones thriving while "degenerate" ones went to the wall....' Savage air quotes made it look as though the DS was skewering Jonathan Warr with each word.

'Well, you can guess what that meant for the learning disabled.'

'Yeah. They'd be institutionalized or sterilized ... or, better still, killed off.' Her hands clenched. 'Fucking *evil*.' Then she went poppy red. 'Sorry, sir.'

'That's all right, Kate. I think we'll find that Doctor Warr liked to imagine he was fighting a heroic battle in the interests of human evolution. Preventing the weak from dragging the strong down to their level.'

'*Sick.*'

'Or being cruel to be kind, depending on your perspective.'

The DI was relieved to see there was no sign of Doyle. After what he had learned from Noakes, he did not imagine the young DC would have much relish for this conversation.

Burton pushed the books to one side as if they were contaminated.

'When we find Warr's killer, there'll be part of me that wants to shake him by the hand.'

'Whatever Doctor Warr's just desserts, Kate, no-one had the right to act as judge and executioner,' Markham said quietly. 'He met a horrible end, and his remains were chucked away like refuse.' The DI was unusually emphatic. '*No-one* had the right to do that to him.'

She bit her lip. 'Yes, sir.' Then, reaching for her notebook, she leaned forward eagerly. 'I think I may have a lead on that patient Rose I was telling you about yesterday.'

'Quick work,' Markham said approvingly.

'A woman at Social Services said there was someone at Mind – you know, the mental health charity – who might be able to help.' A quick check of the notebook. 'Turned out to be a Mrs Margaret Hart ... helps out at the shop in the town centre. She was in there today, so I had a word over the phone. Elderly but still got all her marbles.'

'She knew the family then?'

Markham felt a quiver of anticipation. Of all the histories in those files, Rose's plight stood out as somehow pre-eminently monstrous. And there was that sister who had fought so tenaciously to bring the truth to light ... maybe she held the key.... Currently, it was their best bet. He couldn't go after families from the DCC's list without alerting the powers that be and bringing Slimy Sid down on him like a ton of bricks. Instinctively too, he felt that the roots of Jonathan Warr's murder lay in the distant, as opposed to the more recent, past. Something about the Newman, something in the very fibres of the place, made the DI feel sure their killer had jealously stalked Warr over time, had shadowed him in an intensely intimate and pleasurable pavane, savouring the power of life and death like the doctor's doppelganger. The final act of revenge was probably a downer....

'Mrs Hart remembered the case and kept in touch with Rose's sister Irene while she still lived in Bromgrove. The family name – get this, sir – was Seacombe ... same as those caretakers down at Seacrest.' She sat back triumphantly. 'Bit of a coincidence, boss.'

'I don't like coincidences.' The keen grey eyes turned so stormy, that Burton felt a shiver of fear. The DI was undoubtedly a foe worthy of this killer's steel. Observing that he was deep in thought, she preserved a respectful silence. Had Noakes been able to read Kate's mind while she watched the chiselled features, with as much wonder as though it was Michelangelo's David come to life, he would have arrived at the most alarming conclusions. Luckily for the DS's peace of mind, he was still busy with community relations in the café.

'Right, Kate.' The DS stiffened to attention. 'I need you to visit Mrs Hart as soon as possible. Get everything she can tell you about the family. *Everything.*'

'Do you think this is it, sir?' Burton's voice was hoarse.

'Could well be. At any rate, all the threads lead back to Norfolk.'

Norfolk with its neglected graveyard redolent of secret funeral rites and unrevered remains. Markham felt almost as though he could see right through those makeshift brick vaults, to where tumbled bones waited to be lifted from their dark prison.

'In the meantime, there's the problem of Chief Superintendent Rees whom I happened to see searching Doctor Warr's office just now.'

'*What*! How'd he get in there?'

'I'd rather like to know the answer to that question myself, Sergeant. One of the staff must have given him a swipe card. The question is, who?'

'What're you going to do, sir?'

'Nothing. Rees doesn't know that I saw him. I imagine he'll have rejoined the rest of them in the café by now … I'd better get along and fish Noakes out of there before he spontaneously combusts. After all, there're only so many pies a man can scoff.'

'Well, he'd say he's "keepin' CID's end oop".'

The mischievous mimicry elicited one of Markham's rare charming smiles. It was good to see Burton gradually becoming less po-faced and solemn in his company. On arrival in CID, she'd sounded like a priggish schoolgirl, candidate for Head Prefect no less. But now she felt able to relax and exhibit the puckish side of her personality, he found her quite endearing.

The DI was about to leave the incident room, when he hesitated.

'Did anyone go past here before I came in, Kate?'

'Not that I noticed, sir. On the other hand,' she sounded mildly abashed, 'I was nose deep in Doctor Warr's creepy books.'

Markham frowned.

'Why, boss? Is it important?'

'I don't know,' he said slowly. 'It's just that...' He swallowed what he had been about to say about a face at the window. No need to spook his colleagues with that tale.

'Nothing. Ignore me,' he said abruptly. 'I'll leave you to get that interview sorted. Keep Doyle ringing round agencies ... maybe we can strike lucky with another family.' He paused. 'Where *is* Doyle, by the way?'

'Last thing I knew, he was sorting the time and motion graphs – to show staff and patient movements. Then he said he had a thumping great headache and disappeared.'

Cause and effect, thought Markham wryly. All those coefficients plus Burton reciting chunks from treatises on race science – enough to send anyone reeling.

Noakes was certainly keeping CID's end up, the DI noticed as he slipped back into the café. Muriel had vanished (presumably on smarm patrol elsewhere), which no doubt explained why the DS was now looking more unbuttoned, literally and figuratively. Clearly something of a hit with Linda Harelock and the befrienders, he reluctantly allowed Markham to draw him away.

'Nice woman that,' he said nodding approvingly. 'No side. Told me she's keeping some cake back for that old bugger of a porter cos he never comes to shindigs like this. Too shy.'

'Hmmm. I'm surprised there's anything left,' Markham said, pointedly eying his sergeant's straining waistband.

'Oh yeah,' Noakes said happily. 'My missus bought two of Mrs Harelock's coffee cakes an' all. They won first prize at the Country Fair.'

'Well, when you fail your fitness tests, we'll know who to blame.'

'Oh, I'll get through *those* all right, Guv.' He was the picture

of complacency. 'Piece of piss. Doyle's promised to do some cir-
cuits an' training hooja.... Though I told him straight, I'm not
going to the gym or prancing round in lycra like a nancy boy ...
no way, Jose.'

'Perish the thought,' the DI said faintly. Then, 'Any sign of
the Chief Super?'

'Nah. Jus' showed his face an' chatted up your psychologist
mate.' Noakes's tone was sour. 'Talk of the devil,' he added as
Anna Sladen came over to join them.

'Not interrupting anything, am I?' she said hesitantly.

Noakes drew himself up portentously. Before he could say
'police business' or anything equally fatuous, Markham interposed with 'of course not' accompanied by a welcoming smile.
The DS lurched away, muttering something about checking on
the team, though the gleam in his eye suggested he had spotted
an unattended brownie.

'I don't think I'm exactly flavour of the month with your
sergeant.'

'Don't take it personally, Ms Sladen. He's having difficulty
adjusting to the brave new world of mental hospitals and what
he calls trick cyclists. *Way* out of his comfort zone.'

She gave a throaty laugh. It was disconcertingly seductive.

Again, standing near the psychologist, Markham felt the
tug of attraction. That 'bat's squeak of sexuality', he thought
ruefully, inaudible to any but himself. Or Noakes, he thought
with an inward sigh as he saw the DS glowering from the other
side of the café. Luckily, a couple of befrienders bore down on
him, momentarily eclipsing the beam of disapproval.

The DI and Anna Sladen chatted easily and, for the first
time since the start of the investigation, Markham felt his fraz-
zled nerves start to unsnarl.

It was something about the woman herself. Undeniably

stunning, today she was wearing a simple red jersey dress which clung to every ripe contour but avoided any hint of tartiness. Her thick golden hair, coiled into a French pleat which set off the fine bone structure and sapphire blue eyes, seemed almost too heavy for the graceful neck. Altogether, it was a beautiful composition. As a lonely child, Markham had escaped from the trauma of his domestic circumstances by immersing himself in Camelot, and now it was as though Guinevere or another of his chivalric heroines had miraculously come to life before him. Unlike Olivia's pale pre-Raphaelite allure, with its elusive undertow of something uncanny, there was a serenity about Anna Sladen, like a clear limpid pool which promised the exhausted traveller refreshment and renewal....

She was as caring as she was beautiful, the DI thought while she talked compassionately about Mikey Belcher. He felt a sensation of profound relief that the bereaved man was at last in safe hands.

Noakes suddenly barged into the conversation. 'Sorry to break it up,' he said in an officious tone which suggested he was not sorry at all. 'Your Olivia looked in jus' now.' He waved a meaty paw in the direction of the exit. 'Think she's gone outside.'

'Thank you, Sergeant,' Markham replied coolly. He smiled warmly at the psychologist. 'I've enjoyed our chat, Ms Sladen. Do keep me posted on Mikey. Hopefully I'll be up to see him myself very shortly.'

As he and Noakes walked to the exit, the DI caught a rather unpleasant expression on Sister Appleton's face. As if she knew something to his disadvantage. Doctor Lopez too had been watching closely, but acknowledged the policemen pleasantly enough. Claire Holder, on the other hand, looked as though she had been turned to stone. Markham suspected she had fortified herself liberally beforehand and wondered for the umpteenth time what the woman was so desperate to conceal.

'Kindly stop behaving like a Victorian dowager, Noakes,' Markham rapped when they were out of earshot. As his subordinate's underlip shot out, he added, 'You know *exactly* what I'm talking about.' Uneasily, he wondered how long Olivia had stood unobserved watching him with Anna Sladen.

His girlfriend was sitting on a bench in the little courtyard adjacent to the café, gazing in some bemusement at one of the ubiquitous art installations.

'What's it meant to be, d'you think?' she asked when he and Noakes appeared.

'It's a diving bell,' the DS said proudly as they contemplated the cylindrical cement structure which had a copper lid and porthole on the side. 'No kidding,' he insisted in response to Markham's quizzically raised eyebrows. 'One of them befrienders told me. All the art stuff in this place has summat to do with travel an' voyages, see. So the fruit loops get the idea they're on a journey to recovery.'

'Patients, not fruit loops, Noakes,' the DI intoned with the air of one fighting a losing battle.

'Don't worry, George.' Olivia winked at him. 'I won't tell on you.'

The DS went pink to the tips of his ears. Markham thanked heaven that Muriel Noakes wasn't around to witness her husband's knight-errantry, his weirdly mystical devotion to the DI's girlfriend being something of a sore point. Whatever it was that Noakes saw in Olivia, it had never lost the power to enchant him. Now he was drinking her in with his eyes as though she'd slipped him a love philtre.

'Hop it, Noakesy.' But Markham's voice was kind.

'I'll jus' ...' The DS gestured vaguely at the French windows and betook himself into the corridor, where he mooched back and forth while casting surreptitious peeps at the couple.

For the first time ever with Olivia, Markham felt oddly ill at ease, but he was determined not to show it. He sat down on the bench next to her and took her hands in his.

'Why didn't you come over to me in the café?' he asked gently.

'You seemed otherwise engaged,' came the brittle reply. It did not bode well.

'That was Anna Sladen, one of—'

'I know who she is.' A rush of colour streamed into the pale cheeks. She wrenched her hands away. 'Seems like she doesn't know you're in a relationship.'

'The subject never came up, Liv,' he said quietly. 'I've only seen her a couple of times. On an entirely professional footing.'

'D'you think I'm blind, Gil?' She was fighting back tears. 'I saw the way you were looking at each other.... Another one for you to put on a pedestal....'

'Liv, listen to me.' Markham felt as though the ground was falling away beneath his feet. 'You've got this all wrong.'

'No, I haven't. You need an ideal to worship, don't you, Gil? Something pure and unspoiled ... something to blot out ... what happened to you as a child. Only I can't stay on my pedestal any longer, Gil. It's *killing* me.'

He looked at her in horror. Then he spoke with cold anger.

'This isn't you talking ... this is some psychological clap-trap you're trotting out.'

'Don't be so fucking arrogant.' She flared up. 'I've only just started the regression therapy, and that's got nothing to do with it. This is about me wanting you to accept me as I am. Not your talisman to ward off evil, but the real *me*.'

'I've never seen you in that way.' Markham's voice was flat, almost a whisper.

'Yes, you have,' she insisted wildly. 'And it's distorted our relationship … made it somehow, oh I don't know, *unreal* … like a fairy tale…'

'That's because you haven't been straight with me, Liv. Haven't told me what's wrong.'

'You don't want to hear it, Gil. You just want the mirage.'

Markham exhaled deeply, pale to the lips. On the other side of the French windows, he was aware of the consternation in Noakes's face.

'I haven't got time for all this garbage about pedestals, talismans and … what was it … oh yes,' he almost spat the words, '*fairy tales*. For your information, I'm in the middle of a triple homicide, so spare me.' He gestured to his concerned colleague on the other side of the glass. 'And spare *him* too.'

Her face softened. 'Poor George.'

'Yes. Sometimes I think he's like the child we never had.'

At that, Olivia turned quite white. Stumbling to her feet, she choked, 'I'm going home, Gil. I've had enough.'

A crimson streak came into Markham's face. 'Don't go like this, Liv,' he pleaded.

Shaking her head mutely, she sprang across to the French door and, before he could say another word, she was gone. Noakes stood looking after her, aghast, his face a picture of wretchedness.

'Don't say anything, Noakes,' Markham said through clenched teeth as the other joined him in the courtyard. '*Just don't.*'

And the DS didn't. Instead, almost comically, he showered sympathy and concern out of every pore. Outside Olivia and Noakes, most people found Gilbert Markham diffident, monosyllabic, haughtily reserved (to devastatingly lethal effect in the opinion of Muriel Noakes and sundry other Bromgrove matrons). He did not spread around his affection. He confined it to a few and withdrew from the rest. He was so reclusive, indeed, that it was amazing how quickly he had unbent to George Noakes, a matter of some resentment to the thrusting millennials who hoped to ingratiate themselves with CID's rising star. But, for all the difference in their personalities, Markham knew the big blundering sergeant somehow understood him like no-one else.

Now, the DS just clapped him clumsily on the shoulder. Work, he knew, was the best medicine for his boss.

'Chin up, Guvnor,' he said awkwardly. 'I'll get two cuppas an' we can take 'em back to the incident room.' He jerked a thumb towards the café. 'Leave that lot to their jabbering.'

The DI squared his shoulders. 'Right,' he said, with a desperate attempt at joviality, though he looked stunned, 'let's up and at 'em.'

Silence fell over the little courtyard once more.

The incident room was quiet. No sign of Burton or Doyle. Markham felt almost weak with relief.

As they drank their well-sugared tea (for shock), the DI updated Noakes on Philip Rees's activities.

'Rees'll weasel his way out of it, boss. Say he had permission or summat.' Noakes smacked his lips appreciatively. 'That Mrs Harelock makes a great cuppa.' Then he resumed his previous train of thought. 'The managing director doesn't know whether she's coming or going, Guv, so Rees is on a winner there. She'll agree to whatever he says.'

Markham sprawled dejectedly in his chair.

'What do you think he was looking for?'

'Incriminating letters ... anything that's got his name on it an' links him to dodgy business with Doctor Jekyll.'

'You reckon he was in on it, then?'

'Oh aye,' came the laconic response, 'up to his bleeding neck.' Noakes took a gigantic slurp as though to lubricate the thinking process. 'Look, Guv, whatever Warr got up to in the eighties and nineties with Kennedy and Molloy, by the noughties someone needed to smooth the way, an' who better than Mr Holier-than-thou.'

'You really don't like Rees.'

'Never could stand 'un. Jumps on every band wagon going, but he's not a decent thief taker.'

Podgy fingers drummed on the desk. 'An' 'sides, his eyes are too close together.' Clearly that clinched it.

Markham smiled. Noakes wasn't sure why but felt a glow of pleasure that he had managed to dispel, however briefly, the dreadful lost look in the guvnor's eyes.

The DI felt some of his energy returning. Making a supreme effort to banish thoughts of Olivia, he told Noakes about the potential lead Burton had unearthed.

'The lass done well.' The DS was disposed to be magnanimous.

'I just hope I've not sent her off on some wild goose chase.'

The DS was thoughtful. 'No, it's worth a shot, boss. That Rose's case was worser'n anything else we turned up.'

'A long time to wait for revenge, though, don't you think?' Markham's voice held doubt.

'Mebbe the killer got off on following Warr around ... watching an' waiting,' the DS speculated. 'Or mebbe ... mebbe they didn't have the courage to do owt about Warr, then summat happened to set 'em off.'

The DI thought back to Slimy Sid talking about *folie à deux*.

'*Something or someone.*'

For a while, they sat companionably drinking their tea. Glancing through the window, the DI saw that the January light was already failing, the sun just a dirty yellow blot.

Everywhere was very quiet, as though they were termites at the heart of a great burrow where myrmidons toiled in secret chambers beneath ground. There was a sense of unreality about it all, Markham thought, suddenly light-headed from the strain of his encounter with Olivia.

Later, he couldn't recall how long they had been sitting there when DC Doyle burst into the room as though the hounds of hell were on his tail.

Immediately, the other two were alert, their torpor banished.

'What is it? What's happened?'

The DC looked at Markham, struggling to frame a sentence. Finally, 'Come and see,' he said.

Minutes later they found themselves back in the courtyard next to the café.

'What're you playing at, laddie?' Noakes was brusque. 'There's nowt to see 'ere.'

Then he followed the DI's gaze, which was riveted to the cement diving bell.

Something was pressed up against the porthole.

A dead face.

13

Countdown

MARKHAM STOOD IN OLIVIA'S walk-in wardrobe at The Sweepstakes with his face pressed into one of the jackets his girlfriend had left behind, inhaling the delicate scent of her perfume. The curt note informing him that she had temporarily moved out still hadn't sunk in. At the other end of the apartment he could hear Noakes making a horrible racket as he crashed around making tea and rooting for biscuits, but just for that moment the DI was able to cut off, locked into a secret world which did not connect with his public persona.

The remainder of Saturday had assumed a nightmarish complexion after the discovery of Chief Superintendent Rees's body in the diving bell.

There were no marks of violence on the body, and early indications pointed to Rees having suffered a heart attack. Slimy Sid had swooped on this diagnosis with indecent haste, informing Markham that a press conference would be convened for Monday when the death would be presented as a 'tragic accident unconnected with another ongoing investigation'.

Noakes had been furious. 'Tragic accident, my arse!' he

raged to Markham after they had been dismissed. 'Rees didn't shut himself inside that thing. The lid was closed *from the outside*, for crying out loud.'

'The DCI's following the line that someone saw the lid up and accidentally secured it without realizing there was someone inside.'

'*Bollocks.*' The DS was plethoric with disgust. 'Next thing, he'll be telling us Rees was playing hide an' seek.'

'The Chief Super must've got the idea that Warr had hidden incriminating material in one of the art installations – by way of insurance.'

'But why'd Rees pick that one?'

'His mobile's missing, Noakes. I'm willing to bet he got a text from some pay-as-you-go untraceable telling him to check out the diving bell. Then, he was in such a tearing hurry to get out of Warr's office, that he left his phone behind.'

'But whoever sent that text couldn't count on him leaving his mobile behind.'

'True. Which makes me think this was an impulse kill. Not planned like the others. Whoever lured Rees over to the diving bell saw him in Dr Warr's office, had a rush of blood to the head and took a gamble.'

Noakes whistled. 'Mega risky, Guv. If Rees'd taken the mobile, he might've been able to fetch help.'

'Assuming he could get a signal … but you're right, it was taking a huge chance. The killer couldn't be sure of the outcome – whether Rees would asphyxiate, go into shock, have a heart attack, or end up being spotted and rescued. That's what makes me think this was disorganized … spur of the moment.'

'It went like a dream, though, Guv. I mean, cos the court-yard was at the back of the café, no-one'd think to check it out.'

'How come Doyle was round there?'

The DS shrugged. 'A headache. Couldn't sit still,' he said. Ants in his pants.' A sudden malicious grin. 'An' he'd had an earful.... Burton doing her Doctor Spock bullshit ... prob'ly wanted to get out before he bashed her over the head with one of them textbooks.'

'It must have been a God awful shock. What did you do with him afterwards?'

'Left him with that psychologist woman.' Meaningful pause. 'She said she'd look after him.' The DS shook his head sagaciously. 'The lad'll need counselling like as not. You don't get over summat like *that* in a hurry.'

Rees had apparently climbed down the little metal staircase on the inside of the structure, checking the inner walls for cracks or recesses where paper could be wedged. Tardis like, the sculpture was bigger on the inside than the outside, extending to a depth of several feet beneath the courtyard in which it was embedded. When the lid slammed down and the policeman found himself trapped, he must have panicked. The position of his body suggested he had hoped to attract attention through the porthole, or find an air bubble. Mercifully, it looked as though a cardiac arrest had intervened. His terror inside that cement-rendered iron lung must have been unimaginable. As Markham watched Rees's crumpled body being winched out of the sculpture, the art installation struck him as resembling some surreal version of Little Ease, the windowless cell favoured by medieval torturers, fashioned so that the prisoner within could neither stand nor sit down but was forced to crouch in agony until freed from the suffocating dark space.

The DI had never warmed to Chief Superintendent Philip Rees, an officer he now strongly suspected had helped to dispatch Rose Seacombe and other vulnerable souls to their walled-up repose in the graveyard at Seacrest. And yet, the sight of the strapping detective reduced to a broken marionette filled him with pity and made him even more coldly determined to find whoever had appointed himself judge and jury. Nemesis was at hand, he told himself.

The night is long that never finds the day.

'Guv! Tea's up!' Noakes's stentorian bellow interrupted Markham's reverie.

Gently, he readjusted the hangers in Olivia's wardrobe, as though to convince himself that she would be returning any minute. Then he made his way to the living room.

'I've done you builder's,' the DS said shyly. 'Strong enough to stand a spoon in.'

Indeed he had. And with God only knew how much sugar. The DI's eyes watered.

'Found some biccies too. Reckon your girlfriend,' delicate pause accompanied by a wistful glance, 'won't mind me pinching a few Kit Kats.'

'You know full well she never minds you raiding our stores, Noakesy. Only gets the junk food in for you.'

The DS appeared gratified by this mixed compliment, though he continued to look around anxiously as though he had intuited Olivia's flit. Soon, however, he was happily munching away. Looking up after a few minutes' blissful consumption, he was staggered to see a cigarette dangling from the DI's mouth.

'*I know, I know, Noakesy.*' Markham waved away the anticipated reproaches with an embarrassed air. 'It's just a one-off.'

Noting the exhaustion of the grey eyes embedded in deep dark hollows, the DS said nothing while the guvnor inhaled grimly as though his life depended on it.

Finally, chocolate and cigarette were finished. The two men contemplated each other from the depths of their respective armchairs.

'What do we do now, Guv?'

'We're travelling to Norfolk tomorrow, Sergeant. You, me and Burton. We'll stay the night and come back on Monday.'

The DS sat up alertly.

'Not Doyle?' he said. 'The lad'll be disappointed you don't want him in at the end.'

'Doyle's too fragile. And this is too close to home, Noakes. I'll find a way of making it up to him, I promise.'

'Are we staying in the same place as last time?'

'Yes, though I doubt there'll be much time for Sky in the bar this time round.'

'What's the game plan then?'

'Tomorrow we're going into Diss for a meeting with one of Norfolk Council's Social Care team. After that we'll play it by ear.'

'Oh yeah?' The DS was carefully non-committal. 'Another of Burton's snouts, is it?'

'Not as such.' There were lines of fatigue around the DI's eyes, but they glistened with an inner light. 'Mrs Hart, the lady she spoke to at Mind—'

'The woman who knew Rose Seacombe's family?' Noakes interrupted with quickening interest.

'That's the one. Well, Rose's sister Irene kept in touch and sent postcards from Banham ... that's just six miles from Diss.'

'Irene. Oh yeah.' This had kindled Noakes's interest. 'The stroppy one who tried to blow the whistle on her sicko dad.'

'The very same.' The brooding, penetrating glitter in Markham's eyes intensified. 'It appears Irene took the younger children to live in Norfolk with her after their mother died, and Burton thought they might be on social services' radar – especially if any of the siblings had gone off the rails. With Banham being so close to Diss, she tried South Norfolk Council

191

and struck lucky. They were pretty cagey over the phone, but she's managed to set up an appointment with a family welfare assistant who knows the background.'

'What're you hoping to get from it, Guv?'

'A handle on the family, Noakes.' The DI's long fingers twitched as if he was desperate for another cigarette. 'We need to know the dynamics.' He leaned forward eagerly. 'The answer lies there, I'm sure of it.'

'S'pose we've got nothing to lose,' the DS conceded. 'An' they're likely to wheel on the big guns next week if the case doesn't break soon.'

'Yes.' Markham's voice was bitter. 'The DCI'll scapegoat me into the bargain, I shouldn't wonder.'

'Oh aye, shit runs downhill. That's Sidney's motto all right.' Noakes was philosophical.

The two men sat in silence for a time. Outside, the wind was getting up, soughing and sobbing like the refrain of lost souls cast out from heaven. The sound made Markham shudder.

'I c'n stay the night, if you'd like, Guv. If your Olivia's at her friend's.'

Markham could think of nothing better. He shrank from saying that Olivia had moved out, but Noakes made it seem the most natural thing in the world. And in doing so, with a gentle sensitivity so strikingly at odds with his uncouth exterior, the DS had poured balm upon the wound. The pain was still there, but it no longer smarted as acutely.

'Good idea, Noakesy,' he said hoarsely.

'Right.' The DS rubbed his hands. 'Now that's sorted, what about a takeaway?'

By mutual consent, the subject of the investigation was dropped, and Markham abandoned himself with some relief to his sergeant's idea of a 'lads' night in'.

But the case came back to haunt his dreams in the shape of a withered looking woman, her lips blistered and livid, her hair lustreless, her temples bony and concave. 'I'm Rose,' she whispered. Although the figure stood in a storm-lashed field, not a hair of her head nor a fold of her dress stirred as she looked intently at him. Then the phantom was replaced by Olivia, with a corpse-like pallor, her slim form wrapped in an invisible cloak of aloofness. She was standing on a windy beach, her arms outstretched. 'I'm in a cage, Gil.' The words came from very far away. 'I want to get out. Help me to get out!' Then her face was blotted out by the sun, a huge ball of fire which came dancing out of the sky towards him, whirling like a giant Catherine wheel as though bent on crushing him. He cowered on the ground to get away from it, and when he looked up Olivia was gone.

Markham woke up in the small hours, drenched in sweat.

Logic told him that Seacrest, Holkham Bay, the investigation and row with Olivia were all jumbled up in his mind, triggering the turmoil in his subconscious.

But logic was cold comfort in the circumstances.

His dreams had felt so vivid....

There was no point trying to get back to sleep.

Markham headed for his study by way of the whisky decanter. Pouring himself a generous shot, he hunkered down to await the dawn.

After an artery-hardening fry up the next morning, they were joined by Kate Burton, and the three officers set off in the DI's car. Noakes took the wheel, rear-view mirror carefully angled so he could keep tabs on his fellow DS who sat in the back with Markham.

Somehow Burton managed to tamp down her jealous

curiosity about the DI's domestic arrangements, though her mind teemed with questions. Noakes's air of watchful protectiveness was ample indication that things had gone awry, but she knew better than to raise the guard dog's hackles.

'Seeing as I'm driving, we're not having any of your poncey classical music,' he glowered. 'No way am I listening to Mozart and Beethoven all the way to Norfolk.' Burton had been about to request Classic FM, but decided that discretion was the better part of valour. Smooth was better than nothing.

After an uneventful journey broken only by a 'refuelling stop', they approached Diss. Noakes switched off the radio and the thoughts of all three turned to the case.

'Where do the weirdo bird-watchers fit in, Guv?'

'Bob and Mary Seacombe,' Markham said repressively before pointing out that ornithology was a perfectly respectable hobby. Thoughtfully, he added, 'Presumably Bob Seacombe's related to Rose's father.'

'Oh yeah, the paedo.'

'But it doesn't necessarily mean they're caught up in the conspiracy.'

'You thought there was something a bit off with them, though, didn't you, sir?' Burton prompted the DI.

'They were certainly uncomfortable when they caught us in the graveyard, Kate,' he replied. 'But that could just as well have been because the hospital had asked them to keep it out of bounds to visitors and they were afraid of getting into trouble.'

'But what the heck were they doing there in the first place, Guv?' Noakes was clearly struggling to get his head round the set up. 'I mean, wouldn't they be the *last* people Warr and the others would want nosing around?'

'Could be a guilt-offering,' Markham rationalized. 'They

spun the relatives a line about what had happened to Rose and offered them the position of wardens by way of compensation.'

'A bribe you mean,' Noakes said bluntly.

'More like an *inducement* not to make waves.'

'"Ask me no questions and I'll tell you no lies,"' put in Burton.

'Yes, something like that, Kate. They struck me as timid characters, naturally fearful of those in authority. So, I don't think we're looking at Norfolk's answer to Hindley and Brady.'

'But that's their niece or cousin or whatever chucked out there in that horrible field,' Noakes burst out passionately, red-faced in his outrage. 'Mouldering away without even a bunch of flowers.'

Markham recalled having heard that Noakes belonged to the Bromgrove Cemetery Clearance Association, taking it in turns with other volunteers to tidy neglected plots, clean head-stones and adopt unloved graves. His tone was very mild as he replied, 'They may have been advised an unmarked grave was right in the circumstances ... best not to stir up unhappy memories ... let Rose rest in peace ... publicity a bad thing .... I imagine they'd fall into line pretty quickly.'

'They could have been afraid.'

'That too, Kate. From the conspirators' point of view, it worked out well. They had the Seacombes where they could keep an eye on them.'

'Not all of 'em.'

'True, Noakes. They weren't able to guard against every eventuality.'

Nemesis.

'D'you think the same person killed all four victims, sir?' Burton shot the DI an anxious sidelong glance. 'I mean, the Chief Super's murder doesn't seem to fit the pattern.'

Markham gave a heartfelt sigh.

'As far as the DCI's concerned, it was "accidental death", Kate. Someone shut Rees into that thing by mistake.'

'Accidental death?' She looked startled. 'Have we got any evidence for that?' Her natural deference to authority kicked in. 'Are the facilities people holding their hands up?'

'Of course they're bloody not!' Noakes burst out indignantly. 'Cos it never happened. It's just some cock and bull story designed to take the heat off Sidney. Think about it. Three murders plus a copper. An' not jus' any old copper neither.' His voice was a growl. 'You can bet Ted Cartwright tipped Sidney the wink that we were sniffing round the Chief Super. So he's circling the frigging wagons. Wants to bury the mess six feet deep. Along with Rees.'

'Sir?' Burton looked as though her well-ordered universe was tumbling about her ears.

'I don't believe it was an accident, Kate,' Markham said soberly. 'I think there's something different about the fourth death. The other murders felt calculated, but this was opportunistic ... almost reckless....'

'Are we talking *two* killers, sir?'

'It's possible.'

As Burton digested the implications, Noakes eyed her balefully in the mirror. He just *knew* the daft bint couldn't wait to check it out in one of her creepy books. Probably had one packed for tonight's bedtime reading. *Ugh.*

They were coming into the old centre of Diss. There was the fleeting impression of cottages and town houses interspersed with newly refurbished public buildings. Then it was down a side alley next to the palladian Corn Hall. Consulting her pocketbook, Burton directed Noakes to pull up outside a small gabled building that looked like a converted chapel.

'Doesn't look much like council offices. Are you sure this is the one?'

'Yep. The contact's name is Sarah Davies and this is the address I was given.'

It being Sunday, there was no difficulty about parking. Within minutes they had been whisked upstairs and into a thoroughly modern, light-filled office.

Looking around at the pictures of marinas and boats, Noakes thought they could have been back at the Newman. What was it about the chuffing seaside? He supposed there must be a market for this kind of thing. Artwork for nutters.

While the DS was engaged in these aesthetic reflections, Markham sized up the woman who had ushered them into the building. Petite, with long dark hair and dressed simply in a tunic dress and leggings, she looked absurdly young to be what her lanyard proclaimed her – a family welfare assistant – while the soft accent-less voice suggested she wasn't a native of Norfolk.

Once they were seated in brightly upholstered pine easy chairs and introductions had been made, she offered tea or coffee. Markham swiftly declined, ignoring Noakes's hopeful glances towards the pristine galley kitchen tucked away in an alcove.

'We don't want to take up too much of your time, Ms Davies,' he said cordially. 'It's very good of you to see us at such short notice.'

'Not at all, Inspector.' She hesitated, her manner wary. 'I understand you want to know about the Seacombes in connection with an ongoing investigation?'

Markham flashed Burton a grateful glance. The DS had clearly been circumspect.

'That's correct. Obviously, we can apply for a court order if necessary, but I hope you will take my word for it that this is a matter of some urgency.'

Whatever Sarah Davies saw in Markham's steady gaze seemed to reassure her.

'Irene Seacombe died in 2012, Inspector.'

It was a blow, but Markham had expected something of the kind.

'She'd moved to Banham in 1992 with her three younger siblings.'

'Do you have their names, Ms Davies?' Kate Burton's pocketbook was already open.

'Simon, Gary and Lynsey.'

Something about the names seemed to have arrested Burton's attention. The DI raised an eyebrow, causing her to flush self-consciously. Carefully, in her neat copperplate, she made a note.

'How did they come to your department's attention, Ms Davies?'

'Irene had difficulty coping,' the social worker said frankly. 'Problems with drink and drugs. The kids' schools got in touch over possible neglect, and that's how we became involved. Long story short, Simon and Gary ended up in the criminal justice system, but Lynsey made something of herself in the end. Got six O levels and 2 A levels. According to the files, she did a secretarial course at the Pitman College in Diss before moving away from the area. The three of them would be in their sixties now.'

'You weren't the member of staff assigned to them.'

Cos you look all of ten years old, thought Noakes.

The woman drew herself up as though he had said it aloud.

'That's right,' she said somewhat defensively. 'The staff who dealt with the Seacombes are retired now – their key worker emigrated to Australia – but the details are in the files.' She gestured to a slim manila folder on the coffee table next to her chair. 'I pulled the relevant paperwork when I knew you were coming.'

'Much appreciated, Ms Davies.'

Not by the flicker of an eyelid did Markham show the importance he attached to this interview. Unhurried and imperturbable, there was a stillness about him, a tranquillity which impelled trust.

'Do you happen to know the siblings' current whereabouts?'

The room seemed to hold its breath.

'I'm sorry, Inspector, but that's not in the files.' She sounded genuinely regretful.

'What did the boys do time for, luv?'

'Shoplifting and TWOCing, Sergeant.'

No crimes against the person. No violence.

'Known associates?' This was Burton.

'Oh, they weren't big league. Hung about with some local troublemakers, that was all. Look,' she held her palms upwards in a curiously supplicatory gesture, 'the cards were stacked against them. There'd been some family tragedy which knocked Irene sideways, though they couldn't get her to talk about it. It's a miracle that those kids came out of it as well as they did.'

'What about other relatives?'

'An uncle Robert on the father's side,' came the crisp reply. 'He was Merchant Navy. Married a local girl. I think the family was originally from Norfolk, so perhaps that's why Irene came back in the end.'

'Couldn't the aunt and uncle have helped out with the kids?' Noakes asked. 'I mean, looking out for 'em an' that?'

'Mary Seacombe's nerves were bad,' the social worker replied in a determinedly non-judgmental tone. 'And her husband was away a lot.'

In other words, they were as much use as a chocolate teapot, thought Noakes darkly. No help to those poor kids at all.

'Nerves....' Markham let the word hang interrogatively in the air.

'She had a breakdown, Inspector. I can't recall exactly when this was, but Irene told the key worker her aunt had been treated for clinical depression at some point.'

Jesus, what a family, thought Noakes. Wall to wall whack jobs.

Again, Sarah Davies picked up on the vibrations.

'Fractured lives,' she said. 'We do our best to pick up the pieces.'

'I'm sure you do a good job,' the DI said with obvious sincerity.

She smiled at him, looking very young indeed. 'Thank you, Inspector. Social workers get a rough ride in the press, but if you knew what we're up against....' Suddenly, she blushed. 'What am I saying? Of course you do. We're in the same business after all.'

Yeah, thought Noakes crossly, but we're not feeding the psychos all that BS about not getting enough cuddles when they were little.

Again, from the distinctly hostile glare he received, Noakes had the uneasy feeling Sarah Davies could read his mind. Of course she was coming over all soppy round the guvnor – practically melting into a flaming puddle – while him and DS Swot hardly got a look-in. There was definitely no justice in the world.

Clearly there was nothing else to be gained from the interview. Clutching the manila folder, Markham led his team back to the car.

'Where to, Guv?'

It was still early in the morning and everywhere was very quiet.

A drowsy, unremarkable Sabbath in the little market town.

But they had a killer to catch.

'We'll book into our B&B in Holkham then head out to Seacrest. Bob and Mary Seacombe are worth another crack.' The DI spoke with more assurance than he felt.

'D'you honestly think we'll get anything out of 'em, Guv?' Noakes asked glumly. 'They're a few sandwiches short of a picnic them two. An' if the hospital's said to keep it zipped, there's not much chance they'll cough.'

'We'll have to go in heavy then.' Markham's face had an implacability that his colleagues recognized of old. 'Tell them they may hold the key to *four* murders including a senior police officer.' He added grimly, 'I've a few post-mortem photographs that should help to concentrate their minds.'

'Who's our prime suspect, sir?'

'One of the siblings or someone connected to them.' He spoke authoritatively to disguise the sick hollowness he felt.

'What about the hospital, Guv?' Noakes asked stubbornly. 'Ain't it more likely to be someone there? I mean, say it *is* one of Rose's family behind all of this, how'd they find their way into the Newman?'

'I don't honestly know, Noakesy.' Markham looked round uneasily, as though fearful of being overheard. 'Even since Kate told us about Rose's case history and I saw that abandoned graveyard, I've felt certain the answer lay here.'

Oh no. Noakes's gloom intensified. The guvnor was going all psychic on them. Like when he talked to the dead. Slimy Sid'd do his nut if he heard owt about ghosts and graveyards.

Then the DS clocked miss smarty pants Burton taking it all

in with a furrowed brow. No point letting her see they were up shit creek without a paddle. Markham was his chief always, and that was that. If the DI was making it up as he went along, so what? He reckoned they had twenty-four hours tops before Sidney called in the Yard.

United we stand.

'Right, boss,' he said, starting the engine. 'Mebbe once we bring out the thumbscrews they'll play ball.' With Noakes, the mixed metaphors were a sure sign he was kerflummoxed.

They were just turning into Denmark Street when suddenly Burton exclaimed, 'Stop, Sarge!'

Noakes pulled over. 'What's up?' he rumbled. God, this was all they needed. Burton fannying about on some hairbrained scheme when he was desperate for a cuppa.

'Tell you later.' Breathlessly, she grabbed her shoulder bag and wrenched at the door handle. Over her shoulder, she told Markham, 'I'll catch up with you, sir. There's something I need to do.'

With that she was gone.

'Chuffing Nora.' It was a sigh of purest exasperation. 'D'you want me to hang on in case she comes back, Guv?'

'She's dropped her notebook.' Markham tucked it into his jacket pocket while looking round to see what had attracted his colleague's attention. 'Did you notice anything unusual, Sergeant?'

'Nah.' The DS glanced in his rear-view mirror. 'She dived down one of them ginnels back there like her pants were on fire. Gave me a right turn shrieking like that.'

'No point waiting, since she told us she'd catch up.' The DI's expression was uneasy. It wasn't like Kate Burton to take off. 'I think she saw someone, Noakes.'

It was Noakes's turn to look worried. 'Someone as in a

suspect, boss?' His pudgy features contracted in bewilderment. 'But she doesn't know what them three look like ... Simon, Gary and whatsherface ...'

'Lynsey.'

'Mebbe she saw someone she recognized from the hospital.' The DS thumped the steering wheel as if by that means he could unlock the puzzle.

'I think she saw someone and had a light bulb moment.'

'Eh?'

'She made a connection.'

'Oh aye.' Noakes observed in a tone of profound scepticism. But the note of concern was clear when he added, 'The silly bitch shouldn't have gone charging in there without us. She could get herself into trouble.'

'She's on an adrenaline rush.'

And looking to impress me, the DI could have added. Damn, if he'd only played fair with Kate Burton – let her in more – she wouldn't have felt the need to place herself in danger.

Aloud, he said, 'Let's go straight to Seacrest, Noakes. I've got a bad feeling about this.'

Silently, he sent up a prayer for Burton's safety.

They were in a race against time.

14

Finis

THE QUAINT PASTEL-PAINTED COTTAGES of Diss would normally have pleased the DI, but he was in no mood to appreciate their charm.

Before quitting the town, they drove past the cobblestoned ginnel down which Burton had disappeared. Lined with mews houses, it was just a sleepy-looking little back alley with no distinguishing features. Denmark Street itself was equally unremarkable, only the drab soot-streaked Baptist church standing out from its terraced neighbours.

The January day was fine and crisp, the sun a clear white disc above them – nothing like the fireball of Markham's night-mares. But deep inside, he felt cold fear creeping into his heart as stealthily and remorselessly as one of those sea-fogs that hugged the Norfolk coastline.

Fear for Kate Burton.

And a guilty awareness that she might not have been so impetuous but for a burning desire to gate-crash his fellowship with Noakes.

He had unfairly kept her at a distance, he realized – making her feel there was no room at the table, when all she wanted was a few crumbs.

If she came out of this in one piece, he would bring her in out of the cold. Show her that she was valued..

If …

For all that Burton was his *bête noire*, Noakes was clearly worried too, grinding gears in a manner that Markham would normally have deplored.

'Don't worry, Guv,' the DS said finally. 'We'll find her.' He cleared his throat. 'She's a canny lass when all's said and done.' Markham could only wish she was there to hear the admission. 'She'll play her cards close to her chest.'

'If our killer thinks she's on to him, I wouldn't give much for her chances, Noakes.'

It was a sobering thought which held them in its grip all the way to Seacrest.

The complex itself looked even more forlorn and isolated than on their previous visit, as completely cut off from the world as if it had been a seagoing vessel. The grass-fringed sand dunes, rising and falling in stark monotony only added to this impression, beckoned by the black stretch of water beyond. Even the sun, striking the place, seemed chilled, passing quickly on to Beacon Hill in the distance.

They found Bob and Mary Seacombe in their log cabin. From the apprehension in their faces, it was almost as though they had been waiting for the policemen to return.

Once they were seated around the small office table next to the reception desk, the DI informed the couple without preamble that he was investigating four deaths connected with the Newman Hospital and that it was a murder inquiry.

As he spoke, the life seemed almost visibly to drain out of the wardens till they seemed like husks of the placid retirees who had greeted the detectives on their former visit. Nervously, Mary Seacombe fidgeted with the brittle strands of hair that spiralled untidily from her bun, while her eyes held a look of dull entreaty. Her husband's dry calloused fingers told their own tale as they drummed nervously on the table in front of him.

When he had concluded, the DI's keen grey eyes regarded the pair steadily with an almost magnetic power.

'You need to trust me,' he said quietly, his gaze conveying a meaning beyond the simple words. 'Lives may depend on it.'

One life in particular.

'You had a connection with the Newman Hospital through your niece Rose,' Markham prompted.

'Patrick Seacombe was my older brother.'

The former sea captain's voice had something curiously flat and mechanical in its tone, in marked contrast to the easy rounded countryman's lilt that had fallen so pleasantly on the DI's ear before.

'Pat and I both left home as soon as we could ... our dad ... he abused us, see ...' The words came out in fits and starts. 'I can't talk about it.' Gently, his wife laid her hand on his and the restless drumming stopped.

'I understand.'

Something about Markham's compassionate gentleness broke through the man's painfully erected defences. Almost as though Bob Seacombe knew he was talking to a fellow survivor.

'I went off to sea.' For a moment, he brightened with a glow of reminiscence. 'Later, I heard that Pat had done very well for himself ... started a cleaning company then sold it for a small fortune.' He smiled ruefully. 'I never made a fortune like Pat, but I persuaded Mary to take me on, so I guess I hit the jackpot too.' A soft pressure of her hand on his.

'Did you stay in touch with your brother?'

'No.' He met Markham's eyes. 'We both wanted a fresh start ... too many memories, you see. I went into the Merchant Navy and he moved up north after the old man died.'

'So you never really knew your nephews and nieces?'

'Not to speak of. Mary sent cards for birthdays and Christmas....'

'They kept themselves to themselves, Inspector,' Mary Seacombe put in hesitantly. 'I knew there were problems with Rose ... schizophrenia, Pat said.' Her mouth puckered as though the words were difficult to formulate. 'Irene wrote to me later that Rose had surgery and ended up being put away ... but she said the doctors got it wrong ... she said...' The woman's lips twisted grotesquely.

'Go on, Mrs Seacombe, don't be afraid to tell us everything.'

'Irene said Pat ... interfered with Rosie and got her put away so she couldn't tell.'

She fell back limply in her chair as though aghast at what she had said.

From one generation to the next, thought Markham wearily. Incest and sexual abuse had spread through the family tree like an inherited defect.

'What about the younger kids?' Noakes put in. 'Two boys and a lass, weren't it?'

'That's right. Simon, Gary and Lynsey,' she confirmed faintly. 'Irene brought them back to Norfolk, but I didn't see much of them.' Beads of sweat broke out on her forehead. 'I wasn't myself at the time ... depression.' Brokenly she added, 'I wish now I'd tried harder, but I don't know that it would have made any difference.... Irene went round in a sort of haze ... drink and drugs ... and the kids were out of control.'

'Did Irene want you to help her find Rose?'

'Oh, when she first came down here, she was on and on at me to write to the Health Trust and came out with all sorts of stuff about a cover-up ... about Rose having been locked up to stop her talking.' An ugly flush ran up her neck. 'She even thought Rose could've been kept at Seacrest for a while...' Her voice trailed away into silence. 'Look, Inspector,' she said miserably, 'Irene was paranoid. Saw conspiracies everywhere.'

'Didn't you think it strange that no-one ever knew Rose's whereabouts?' Markham put in.

'There was a care plan in place ... Pat decided to leave it to the professionals ... it meant the family could get on with their lives.'

'Not Rose's mum, though,' Noakes said bluntly.

'Anne had been ill for a while. She took what happened to Rose very hard.'

'Your brother-in-law didn't try to stop Irene upping sticks with the younger kids?'

'No, Inspector. I suppose he was tired of all the drama and thought a fresh start all round would be best.' Through stiff lips she added, 'Something went out of him after Anne died. Then their eldest boy, Andrew, was killed in a car crash which pretty much finished him off.'

'Pat was a broken man when he died,' Bob put in. 'Whatever happened with Rose, believe me, he paid for it.'

The expression on Noakes's face suggested this was open to doubt, but he said nothing, sympathy for the man's obvious distress restraining his tongue.

'I believe there was another older brother.'

'Yes, Inspector. Neil.' Mary Seacombe answered the question as her husband appeared beyond speech. 'He died of cancer two years ago. Neither Andrew nor Neil had a family.' The woman looked worn, tired and pathetic. 'We didn't really know the older boys at all,' she said through bloodless lips. 'Pat didn't welcome interference ...'

'You don't have to justify yourselves to me, Mrs Seacombe.' Markham's voice was unusually soft. 'Other people never really know the truth of what goes on in families.'

God knows they didn't with mine.

Something in the DI's serene assurance must have communicated itself to her. Sitting up straighter, she managed a tremulous smile.

'How'd you end up managing this place?' Casually, Noakes brought her back to the Newman.

'Oh, it was just one of those unlikely coincidences,' she said timidly. 'One of the consultants who treated Rose remembered me from one of the letters I'd written for Irene after she moved back to Norfolk. I heard from him out of the blue about a year and a half ago. The hospital was looking for caretakers for this place, and he wondered if we'd be interested. Bob had left the Navy and we were looking about us, so it came at just the right time.'

'Who was the doctor, luv?'

'A Doctor Warfield.'

Bob Seacombe found his voice. 'No, it was Doctor Warr, Mary.'

'Sorry, yes, that's right. Doctor Warr.' She sounded flustered. 'It was a terribly nice letter.... Obviously, he couldn't go into Rose's case cos of patient confidentiality and all that. But he said he remembered the family and wanted to do something.'

She looked at the two men, nervously pleating her skirt. 'I've still got the letter somewhere ... I could look it out if you like.'

'Thank you, Mrs Seacombe.' Markham was very calm. 'As I said, our investigation relates to the Newman, so anything you can tell us will help.'

'You said it was murder.' Her voice was very small. 'Is Doctor Warr ... I mean, did someone...?'

'He's one of the victims, yes.'

She looked stunned and, suddenly, very scared.

Bob Seacombe rose awkwardly to his feet. 'Go and fetch the letter, Mary. I'll make us some tea,' he said, gesturing to the back of the cabin.

'Good idea,' Noakes said heartily. He turned to Mary. 'By the way, luv, if you've got any photos of the family, that'd be a help too.'

The two Seacombes pattered off on their various errands.

As the two policemen watched them go, their faces were wiped clean of sanguine assurance and cheerful bonhomie.

'So Warr got in touch,' Noakes hissed. 'Squaring Rose's folks.'

'Yes, with the GMC and the rest starting to take an interest, he must have wanted to make sure the Seacombes knew which side their bread was buttered. He couldn't leave anything to chance. The troublesome sister was dead, but who knows what she might have told the aunt....'

'D'you think they realized Rose likely ended up in that horrible graveyard?'

In his mind's eye Markham saw the rain-drenched field and a rough, plank bier with a cheap plywood coffin resting on it; saw the weazened little corpse, bruised like a forceps baby, lowered into its brick prison.

'I think subconsciously they knew, Noakes.' A strange faraway look entered his eyes. 'I think they've always known. But they couldn't face the truth, and denial became a way of life... It was too late to put things right, so they took what was offered and made the best of it.'

With the strange empathy that existed between them,

Noakes knew instinctively that the guvnor was thinking of his own past on which the veil was rarely lifted.

The DI gave him a wry smile. 'Good call about the photos. There aren't any in that file from the social worker.'

Restlessly, the DS got up and wandered over to the reception desk, idly flicking through the pages of the visitors' book.

Suddenly, he stiffened as though transfixed.

'What is it, Sergeant?'

'Oh God,' the other stammered.

Markham rose, alarmed. His rubicund sergeant had turned quite grey.

'Jesus, Mary and Joseph.' The DS looked as though he might keel over. 'It's been right under our noses all the time. An' Burton must've twigged ... must've seen...'

He was gabbling now. 'Gimme her pocketbook, Guv.'

Almost snatching it out of Markham's hand, he rifled through the pages muttering to himself. 'She was doodling in that social worker's office ... scribbling summat.'

'Noakes, you're not making any sense.'

The DS found what he wanted and crowed exultantly as he shoved the open pages and visitors' book at Markham, '*Look, Guv, look!*'

In an instant, the DI understood, and it was as though every drop of blood in his body congealed at the discovery.

At that moment, Mary Seacombe came in with some photographs. With nerveless fingers, Markham spread them out on the table.

'*There, boss!*' Noakes said hoarsely. '*There at the back!*'

Mary Seacombe looked from one to the other with frightened eyes.

'What is it?' she whispered.

Bob Seacombe had rejoined them with a tray of tea and

biscuits which he set down, unheeded, beside them.

'Mr Seacombe,' Markham's voice was urgent. 'Last time we visited, you told us that field round the back of the complex was out of bounds.'

'That's right. There used to be a church there too, but it's long gone.' The man leaned against the table as though for support.

'You said you meant to put up a notice, but hardly anyone ever came.'

'That's right.' The man's eyes were wary.

'Had there been trouble with trespassers, then?'

'There was the odd prowler. Nothing to speak of, though.'

The odd prowler.

'You found something in the field?'

'Some ribbons ... trinkets ... children's toys ... and from time to time there were flowers.'

'Someone was visiting it?'

'So long as they weren't doing no harm, we turned a blind eye.'

'There was never any vandalism or anything like that,' his wife said hastily.

'I reckon they'll come back here, Guv.' Noakes bounced agitatedly on the balls of his feet.

'Please.' Mary Seacombe touched Markham's sleeve. 'What's this all about?'

Gently pressing her into a chair, Markham told her.

'Hello there! I never expected to see you here!'

As soon as the words were out of her mouth, it felt like a mistake. Too falsely bright.

'Oh, I'm from round these parts, Sergeant. I thought you knew.'

Burton swallowed. She'd got away with it.

'I'm parked just round the corner, if you'd like a lift somewhere.'

A vision of the DI swam in front of her eyes. Of Markham smiling at her ... congratulating her ... letting her into the circle of intimacy he shared with Noakes ... an outsider no longer.

'Sure, why not?'

But then, when the car door locks clicked and she glanced sideways at the driver's profile, she realized with a sinking heart that she hadn't got away with it after all.

'You know who I am, don't you, Sergeant?'

The voice was unrecognizable.

Play dumb. Play for time.

'I don't know what you mean.'

'Yes, you do. I saw it in your face back there.' Narrowed eyes. 'Don't take me for a fool.'

A glint of metal from the knife held below the steering wheel. To a passerby, they would look like two friends having a chat.

Numbly, she nodded.

Linda Harelock smiled amiably, for a moment transformed into the good-natured bustling creature of their first encounter. The switch was chilling.

'Sensible girl. Sergeant Noakes tells me he fancies you're so sharp you'll cut yourself.' The smile didn't reach her eyes. 'Well, we don't want blood all over my nice clean upholstery, do we?'

'Why did you do it, Lynsey?'

'Don't call me that.'

'All right then, Linda.' Burton felt as though her heart must explode out of her chest, so violent was its pounding. 'I think I know why Doctor Warr had to suffer. But what about the rest? Why did they have to die?'

'I can't tell you here. There's somewhere I need to be.'

Unlike the motherly warmth of the woman's usual tones, her voice was now eerily monotone, devoid of light and shade, as though ventriloquized from outside herself.

'All right.' Burton fought for calm. 'I'll go wherever you like, hear whatever you want to tell me.'

The other started the engine and the car picked up speed.

Burton thought about trying to grab the wheel and decided against have-a-go heroism.

Perhaps Linda Harelock *wanted* to hand herself in after so many years of living a lie....

Seacrest.

Burton recognized it from the DI's description.

God, it was a soulless place, she thought, as Linda Harelock led her to a gully which dipped down at the far end of the abandoned graveyard on the side closest to the road.

Pressing the policewoman to the ground, the knife at her throat, the erstwhile befriender hunkered down next to her. As if they were two schoolgirls playing truant, thought Burton with rising hysteria.

'No-one can see us down here,' Linda said with satisfaction. 'But I'll know if anyone comes this way.'

The gully felt unpleasantly dank, but Burton barely noticed. She waited to hear the truth.

'I watched out for my sister Rose when I was a little girl,' came the whisper in her ear. 'Even though she was older than me. I played with her ... helped her to spell and count.' There was a momentary catch in the rasping voice, then the other continued. 'She was very pretty and always smelled of lily of the valley ... Mum used to give her dabs of perfume for a treat ... she loved that.'

'What was wrong with her?'

'She was just slow, that's all. They'd call it learning difficulties now. Me and Mum helped her keep up. And she was happy with us.' Another painful sound as though Linda was trying to swallow past a lump in her throat. 'Then one day she was gone and I never saw her again.'

'Did anyone ever talk to you about it?'

'No, but I came across Mum crying. Irene, too.' Again, that working of the throat. 'It must've been after they found out what those bastard doctors had done to her. I heard Irene talking about it one day when she didn't think I was listening. Rose flew at her with her fists when Irene went to see her in hospital and then she wouldn't look at her at all.' Linda crumbled damp soil between her fingers, oblivious of the dirt. 'At the back of her poor damaged mind must've been the thought that she had had this surgery and no-one showed up.'

Burton momentarily lost her fear listening to this horror beyond horror.

'Your mum never spoke out?'

'She repressed it, like she repressed the whole disaster of her marriage and what ... Dad ... did. She repressed it all and pretended that it had never happened and that Rose no longer existed.' Linda gave a mirthless laugh. 'There were so many secrets, you see. Not just with Dad ... but my older brothers too. We had to learn not to see.... It killed Mum in the end.'

'Irene fought for Rose, didn't she?'

'Huh. Much good it did her. They were too strong for her. Sent her round the twist like Mum. She got us younger ones out of there, but after that she fell apart. It was the end of us as a family.'

'I'm so sorry.'

'Save your pity, Sergeant. We got Doctor Warr in the end.'

We.

Before she could gather her wits, the woman was talking again, an enigmatic smile playing about her lips as if the encircling band that had bound her brain for so many weary years had suddenly snapped to give her peace of mind.

'You wanted to know why the others had to die, Sergeant.' A crafty expression came into her eyes, so that it was as if a demon suddenly peered out from behind the befriender's pleasant unremarkable exterior.

'Hayley got nosey, I'm afraid. I'd left my locker open, you see, and she just couldn't resist taking a peep.' Her tone now mildly regretful, she explained, 'There were some documents in the name of Lynsey Seacombe plus some of Irene's original correspondence with the Newman. I shouldn't have kept the letters there, but I liked to have them near me as a reminder. It took me so long to build up the courage ... so many years of watching and waiting ...' Stalking Jonathan Warr in the guise of the friendly volunteer. Part of the hospital's furniture. Safe and unthreatening. Until things fell apart.

'Hayley tried to blackmail you.'

'She wanted to better herself ... travel. That waste of space boyfriend at the *Gazette* opened her eyes to other possibilities than being a put-upon receptionist. She was a sharp little thing all right – had her ear to the grapevine, knew all about the rumours of abuse ... when she worked out who I was, she made the connection with Doctor Warr's murder and tried to use it to her advantage. Poor stupid little girl.' It was an unsettling echo of Noakes's words when he found Hayley's body.

'And David Belcher? Had he discovered your identity as well?'

'No, nothing like that.' She flashed a coy smile, and again it was as though the demon unveiled itself.

'He used to go jogging round Bromgrove Rise and saw us up there. Dumping the body, only he didn't realize it at the time. Later, after Doctor Warr was found, it fell into place.'

Us.

Take it slowly, Burton.

'Did David want money too?'

'No, he was on an ideological crusade. Thought he could ... *persuade* me to pass on information from inside the Newman. He wanted stuff he could use against the hospital.' There was an almost petulant edge to her voice, and the strangely artful look returned to her face as she insisted. 'I couldn't take the risk of him talking. We weren't finished.'

We.

'Was someone else—'

But Linda was looking up the bank to the top of the gully where a figure was silhouetted against the sky.

Burton followed the woman's gaze.

The kindly face of Ernie Roberts, the head porter at the Newman, looked back at her.

'Oh, Mr Roberts,' the DS exclaimed, 'thank God you're here. I need help.'

Then, suddenly, she registered the meaning of his presence.

Linda Harelock had said she needed to be somewhere.

We. Us.

She had met the porter there *by appointment.*

Burton's eyes filled with a mounting horror which dilated her pupils until the pair before her blurred together.

Linda clambered up the gully, forcing the policewoman in front of her, the wicked little knife once more at her throat.

'It's over, luv.'

The hand holding the knife shook uncontrollably.

'I couldn't help it, Ernie. When I saw that policeman in

Warr's office, I just lost it … don't know what came over me.…
I just wanted to punish them … get my own back on the lot of
them.' Her voice was ragged with desperation. 'You do understand, don't you?'

'Course I do, luv.'

The tenderness in his eyes was a revelation.

God, these two were in a *relationship*. In it together.

'But it's all over now, Lin.'

He pointed across the field to a cluster of dark figures.

'The police are here,' he said softly. His eyes met Burton's.
'Your fella's come for you.'

Markham. Burton's heart gave a great leap of joy.

The knife wavered, but this time Linda Harelock's voice
was strong. 'I'm not leaving here, Ernie. I'm not leaving Rose.
They're never putting me in a police cell.'

An unspoken message seemed to pass from one to the other.

The man took two swift steps towards them.

There was the flash of metal and Burton recoiled, but it was
the other woman's blood which drenched her.

The last thing she saw before passing out was Markham's
dark, eager face, clean cut against the January sky where the
winter sun throbbed red like burning charcoal.

EPILOGUE

'I STILL CAN'T BELIEVE it, sir. I mean, *Ernie Roberts*! Looked like he wouldn't hurt a fly.' DC Doyle shook his head in stupefaction.

'Ex-Army,' grunted Noakes. 'Still waters an' all that.'

Markham nodded. 'There was much more to Mr Roberts than met the eye.'

Boundless rage against the doctor who had poisoned his wife's peace with pharmaceuticals and dubious therapy, so that she never fully recovered from the nervous breakdown which forced her to give up work and become a recluse. The head porter, rightly or wrongly, blamed Jonathan Warr for her decline, and the doctor's arrogant demeanour merely served to fan his hate.

There was self-hatred too.

'Doctor Lopez says Ernie was only able to cope with Doctor Warr's murder by dissociation – blotting it out. So that when he "discovered" the body, he genuinely had temporary amnesia, though his memory gradually returned along with all the horrific details like the mutilation.'

'Sounds like you're saying he had PTSD, sir.' Doyle was curious.

'I imagine his defence team will use it at trial.' Markham smiled at the detective's interest, relieved to see that his recent gloom had lifted.

The three men were sitting in the back room of The Grapes, enjoying the pub's snug warmth and a crackling fire. They had the place to themselves, Denise the landlady having declared it out of bounds to her regulars who accepted the blatant favouritism with philosophical resignation. Denise was not a woman to be trifled with.

'Roberts knew what he was doing when he killed the rest, though,' Noakes said belligerently.

Markham savoured his Hendrick's before replying.

'True, Noakesy. You were the one who pointed out that Hayley looked as though she was tucked up in bed … posed like a Disney princess … like the murderer cared for her.'

'S'right.'

'Well, I should have taken more notice. Ernie and Hayley were friends, you see. Linda Harelock told us that Hayley walked his dog and dropped in to see him.'

'Which explains the way we found her.'

'Exactly, Doyle.'

Noakes looked mollified. Then his face fell. 'The DCI was on to summat when he spouted all that *folie à deux* stuff. We'll never hear the bleeding end of it.'

'Oh yes.' Markham grinned. 'He'll be pluming himself on that psychology degree every chance he gets … especially when the cameras are around.'

'Who'd have pegged Linda Harelock and Ernie as lovers, though? I mean, they're ancient.' Doyle's bemusement was profound.

Noakes did a protracted eye roll.

Markham laughed. 'Putting sex aside, they'd both suffered at the hands of the medical profession. It was only when Linda got together with Ernie that she found the strength to take her revenge on Jonathan Warr.' His face darkened. 'I imagine she was the one who initiated the mutilation, even if she didn't wield the knife herself.'

'She was out of it at the end, Guv.' Noakes's mind had travelled back to those final moments at Seacrest.

The DI murmured his agreement. 'Yes, she'd had enough. She knew she'd never survive a prison sentence.' He took another cool draught of Hendrick's. 'I think she wanted Ernie to kill her.... Both their hands were on the knife, and Burton thought some sort of signal passed between them at the end.'

'How's Burton doing, sir?' Doyle asked awkwardly.

'Taking it easy for the time being,' came the easy reply. 'But you know Kate,' he added sardonically, 'she won't be able to keep away from the pair of you for long.'

'I thought she was a goner when I saw them doodles ... Lynsey ... Lyn ... Linda...and realized who she'd gone after.' Noakes gave a convulsive shudder. 'Harelock had written it in the visitors' book too, bold as brass ... scouting the place out without her own flesh an' blood being any the wiser.'

Markham said nothing about the way Burton had looked at him before the rest of them reached her – the unforgettable expression in her eyes. That was between the two of them.

He remembered, also, the big, clumsy bear hug that Noakes had given his terrified colleague before she was led away. That, too, spoke volumes.

'What's going to happen to Claire Holder an' Cartwright, Guv?'

'Well, you'll have heard the saying "The wheels of justice turn slowly, but grind exceedingly fine."' Markham looked into the fire's leaping flames as if picturing the future. 'I feel sure the law will catch up with them in the end.'

'Let's hope it's some time this century,' grumbled Noakes.

'Will DCI Sidney authorize the exhumations in that

graveyard now, sir?'

'Once the publicity dies down, yes, Doyle.' Markham thought of all those Norfolk suns that had risen over Rose Seacombe's head and set at her feet. 'There'll be proper funerals too for all who "disappeared".'

Noakes was pleased. 'Mebbe we c'n see about tidying the place up ... lay a few flowers an' all.'

'I'll make it your responsibility, Noakesy.'

'There's going to be a joint funeral service for Hayley Macdonald and David Belcher,' Doyle said.

It felt somehow appropriate. Two young lives snuffed out before their time in the shadow of the Newman.

'We'll be there,' said Markham.

Later, after Doyle had left them for football practice, Markham and Noakes sat together, lazily disinclined to move.

'I heard on the grapevine the Chief Super was seeing that psychologist bird.' The DS paused portentously. 'Like dating her.'

'A man of excellent taste if nothing else.'

Noakes appeared less than satisfied with this rejoinder.

'D'you think she had any idea what he was mixed up in?'

'I very much doubt it,' came the tranquil reply. 'That's a woman who cares for her patients.'

And with that the DS had to be content, though he hummed and hawed till Markham decided to put him out of his misery.

'I'm seeing Olivia later tonight.'

'Champion, Guv.' He beamed.

Markham's hand, unseen, caressed the mobile in his pocket with its precious message. Tonight they would talk and all the ghosts would be laid to rest.